I0699537

Disposable Magic

Dani Finn

DRAGONHEART PRESS

Content warnings

This book is intended for **adult audiences** and contains sex scenes involving magical cephalopods.

ONE

Cliff made his way down the narrow walk of slippery cobbles that ran under the bridge. Muddy stains along the cracked walls lining the Trench showed that low tide would hit within a bell and a half. He uncoiled his skimnet, which was held together by countless twisted pieces of wire salvaged from an even older one, but worked well enough. He scanned the water as he approached the first outflow and saw exactly what he'd expected: swarms of silversides moving and flashing in hypnotic patterns, hovering just below where the clear water entered from the power plant. He gazed into the murky water downstream, studying the surface for signs of anything larger, but the water was lazy and calm.

Another skimmer had disappeared by the next out-flow downstream a few weeks before, and the blood-stains still darkened the cobbles. The constables de-cided he'd been murdered and dumped into the water, but none of the skimmers and scavengers who worked the Trench believed it. Louie didn't have any enemies, or any money for that matter, and his skimnet had been found mangled at the bottom of the Trench. Some kind of giant snake or eel was the prevailing theory; a skimmer claimed to have seen one engulf a leathered turtle the size of a man near the third out-flow. Cliff had seen plenty of strange things in the wa-ter, but never anything bigger than mouthfish, which could grow larger than a man but were harmless as babies.

The water had changed, Cliff thought as he crouched above the outflow. Ever since the pow-er plant had opened two years ago, species like the silversides, which he hardly ever used to see in the Trench, now proliferated downstream from the plant. Mouthfish were becoming scarce, and turtles too. A lot of skimmers wouldn't work at night, even on the outgoing tide when the dwemer was strongest. Cliff got the creeps in the daytime, too, after what had happened to Louie.

He scanned the water downstream one more time just to be safe, then lowered his skimnet into the water. It tangled for a moment, then flexed into a triangle as the weights caught. Cliff studied the taut steel-laced cord as it vibrated in the current. He felt the faint buzz of the handle as the reservoir began to fill. It would take a while, especially since his reservoir had a hairline crack in the glass and didn't get perfect suction. He had more time than marks, so he held the skimnet steady, hoping to get enough dwemer to make it worth the trip before the constables chased him off. He pulled a half-smoked cheroot from behind his ear and carefully lit a match, bracing the skimnet handle against his hip. He'd just managed to light his smoke and suck in a harsh lungful when he saw it.

At first, he took it for a large mouthfish, but it was darker, and it moved in odd pulses through the muddy water. As it entered the clearer water near the outflow, Cliff could tell it was no fish, nor any other creature he'd ever seen in the Trench. Its head and body were oblong, and it trailed a mass of tentacles behind it, with two more that ended in soft, leaf-like pads exploring the water ahead of it. The school of silversides moved in coordinated patterns surely designed to confuse it.

The creature stopped, front tentacles waving in the current. Its dark body flashed white for an instant, and the entire school of fish stopped moving and began drifting toward it. Its skirt flowed around front, spreading wide like a funnel. The two front tentacles swept the dead or stunned fish toward its beak, which snapped shut, leaving only a few fish floating awkwardly downstream behind it. Its rear tentacles snatched them from the water and fed them to its mouth, which opened just wide enough to suck them in.

The handle had just started to warm in Cliff's hand, so the reservoir was roughly a quarter full. He could try to reverse the flow and send the dwemer back into the water in a concentrated burst, which might stun the creature. Or piss it off enough that it would climb up the wall and do him like it had done Louie. And losing the dwemer would mean another day of thin soup at the Works House and put him no closer to a new skimnet. He held perfectly still, ignoring the cheroot smoke stinging his eyes and the roiling terror in his gut, and waited.

The creature approached the skimnet, the two front tentacles hovering near it but not touching it. A smaller creature, which Cliff took for a fish at first, darted out from among its rear tentacles and zipped forward, moving along the outer lines of the skimnet. Its tentacled body flashed a bewildering pattern of bioluminescent colors, then quickly returned to its dark state. The larger creature responded with its own series of colors on the widened ends of its front appendages, and the little one darted back over to it and disappeared into the tentacles at its rear.

It turned slightly, fixing Cliff with one large, unblinking eye, yellow with a wide black stripe in the center. He grew dizzy for a moment, then the creature turned away from him, rotating with the help of its tentacles, and disappeared in a cloud of muddy water. He followed the ripples of its wake with his eyes until they vanished about fifty spans downstream.

Cliff sucked hard on his cheroot, then blew out a long cloud of smoke, which drifted down toward the Trench. He stubbed the remains with trembling fingers, then stuck it back behind his ear. His legs were cramped from squatting, but he couldn't find the strength to stand or sit, so he remained as he was, struggling to catch a breath as he pictured the creature's terrifying beak opening wide to engulf the school of tiny fish, the roiling mass of its tentacles, the unearthly intensity of its gaze.

"Find your way through the chaos," he mumbled to himself, repeating the storm shaman's mantra. It had been a long time since he'd been in the right headspace to practice, but he drew his attention back to the skimnet's cord, which vibrated ever so gently from the current's pull. He let that hum flow into him through the handle, which was warming nicely as dwemer flowed into the reservoir, and his body released its tension in an instant. His breathing steadied and his mind cleared.

Whatever the creature was, somehow living in this channel of Umian's wastewater, it had left him alone. The constables hadn't poked their noses under the bridge either, and the reservoir had to be over fifty percent by now. The plant was kicking out more dwemer than usual today, and it seemed a waste to let it flow out into the bay and be absorbed by jellyfish. A full reservoir, or as full as his would get with its crack, would see him through the better part of a week if he stayed frugal.

He relit his cheroot, staring at the brown water fading to black as it disappeared into the shadows under the bridges.

They only gave him seventy percent credit at the recharge, blaming him for the cracked reservoir, unswayed by his statement that it was cracked when he got it. In the end, he permitted the theft because he had no alternative. He spent an extra-long time examining the new reservoir to make sure they couldn't steal from him this particular way next time. He still gave the serviceperson a quarter-mark tip; they could have ripped him off worse, and he'd probably have to do business with them again.

He slipped the fourteen marks onto his clip and screwed it tight, then let it drop on its sturdy little chain into his pocket. It would take a determined thief to wrench his belt off to steal a few paltry marks, but times were hard. He kept a sharp eye out as he made his way through the lower city, still stinking from the last time the Trench had overflowed. He'd managed to get his tent wrapped up and his trunk onto high ground just in time, but those who lived in the warren of ramshackle wooden structures spreading out from the lower Trench had to live with the stench for a few weeks several times a year. Some of his fellow skimmers were talking about building a shack of their own along one of the smaller canals closer to the plant, but Cliff had his sights set upstream.

He bought a pair of sausage rolls, one for dinner and the other for breakfast, and a bottle of gutter wine to wash it down, then found his way through the maze of tents to his modest tarp cubicle. The sky was an ashen gray, spitting raindrops in uneven bursts. Cliff tightened the cords and straightened the sandbags that kept his floor mostly free of runoff in anything but the biggest storms.

This sky was capable of anything, but his gut told him it would just be a daylong drizzle. The front flaps were still tucked under the sandbags, and the dingy blue ribbon still held the entrance closed. He pocketed the ribbon, breathing a sigh of relief when he glanced inside and saw nothing had been touched. Folks were usually good about keeping an eye out for each other, but thieves were equally good at avoiding detection, so every day was a gamble.

He begged a cup of tea off Mae Kambal, who always had a little pot going. Her son brought her a bag of charcoal pellets every week, tiptoeing through the muck and detritus of the camp paths in shiny leather shoes and a shirt with ruffles. They'd sit on the porch of her shack drinking tea and talking about work, politics, and the weather; he always greeted Cliff with an untroubled uptown smile. The lower city was dangerous for its inhabitants, but everyone knew the constables would exact cruel punishments if anything happened to an uptowner here; their batons would not fall on the criminals alone.

Cliff sipped his tea and settled down on his bedroll, keeping the front flaps open for light to read by until the wind-driven drizzle started dampening his sheets. He secured the flaps and turned the knob on his cell lamp, which provided a pale, flickery light, barely enough to read by, but easy on the dwemer.

He'd found one of the latest issues of *Savage Adventures* under a bench in the park, and he gnawed on a sausage roll as he reread the story of a muscle-bound warrior and her scout, a slender elfin figure who could turn into a cat. They were seeking a stolen sword of great power held by a group of lumbering ogres who slept the day away and ransacked the countryside by night. The prose was nothing special, but the fight scenes were exciting, and the little hints of romance between the two companions had him doing mental gymnastics trying to figure out how he could afford the next issue, which would come out at mid-cycle.

When he finished the slim volume, he did his ablutions and flipped off the lamp, leaving him in near darkness. The rain grew steadier as evening turned to night. Water streaked across the ground, flowing into the little Y-shaped channel he'd dug for drainage. The deep howl of the warning siren vibrated his very bones, and he imagined the boats hurrying back toward the docks as the incoming tide met the swelling Trench, creating a maelstrom of wild currents. Somewhere out there, hidden beneath the murky surface, swam a tentacled creature that could change colors at will and stun anything in the water around it: a creature big and strong enough to pull a person into the Trench and have its way with them.

A creature like that had to have come from the sea. But why was it here? Was it after something larger than silversides? Cliff patted his clip of coins, still secure on its chain in his pocket. He wouldn't need to get close enough to the Trench to find out for a few days at least, which would give him time to see if he could use his outdated university card to get into the Hilltop library. It all depended on who was at the desk and how busy they were. Whatever this thing was, it had to be in one of the illustrated encyclopedias there. And with any luck, he might come across something about a fifty-span-long snake that could swallow a leathered turtle in one gulp.

He drifted off, half-expecting to be devoured by a giant sea monster in his dreams. Instead, it was the diminutive tentacled creature that visited his sleeping mind, flashing mesmerizing color patterns whose meaning eluded him.

Two

Sef swam slowly toward the drop-off with Kin in her skirt. She wondered about the human's net, which seemed to filter dwemer from the clear-water source. It tasted exactly the same as what had come out of their home vent deep in the bay until the humans capped it a year ago. Though some dwemer still filtered out from small holes here and there, it wasn't enough to go around, and territorial battles had erupted for the little corners of the reef that still had enough to support life. Even there, the tiny hexies at the base of the food chain were being wiped out as soon as they hatched. It was a catastrophe.

Some of their kind had migrated to deeper vents, but Sef didn't relish the idea of trying to oust another cuttler from its home or risking being devoured by the ravagers that had followed their migration. A few of the giant predators remained in the deeper part of the bay, but they had expanded their range looking for food; she'd even seen one inside the channel the humans had squeezed the river into to make room for their sprawling habitat.

Sef dipped below the lip of the drop-off, sending out a sounding pulse in all directions to scan for ravager energy signatures. She found nothing except schools of smaller fish and a pair of mouthfish feeding in the kelp beds below. She descended into a patch of kelp and opened her skirt. Kin flitted out, pausing in front of her to express his excitement in a series of colored flashes.

"They didn't seem very afraid of us," Kin said hopefully, projecting an image into her mind of the figure crouched above the river with the strange net.

"They were probably too terrified to move."

"I don't know. I think they were curious." Kin always thought the best of others, which was as cute as it was dangerous.

"I think you're the one who's curious."

"Aren't you?" Kin flashed an exuberant array of colors, flitting in erratic patterns between her front tentacles. *"I mean, that dwemer net they had was pretty interesting. Not the most efficient thing I've ever seen, but for an airlocked creature, they seem quite inventive."*

"Kin, these are the same humans that hunt us for sport. The same humans that capped the vent, stole the dwemer, and forced us to their filthy river for scraps."

"I don't know. It seems like that one was living off the scraps, same as us. Maybe they're fighting for resources too." He wiggled into her right pad, which she half-closed around him as she began to move; he liked to be able to see where he was going. She powered them down into the abyss with easy pulses, now that they were in clean water again with enough oxygen to breathe. Sef felt the first tingles as her stomach began digesting the fish, releasing a low, steady stream of dwemer into her blood. Kin snuggled in, flattening himself against her pad and milking one of her ducts, which warmed at the connection.

"Mmmm." Kin's satisfaction filtered into Sef, who squeezed him just a little tighter. *"Thank you."* His

tiny tentacles wrapped around the base of the duct, caressing it with gentle strokes.

"Not while I'm swimming, love." She cut off the stream for a moment, and Kin sent her mind a dim blue color, which lightened as she opened up again.

"I just want to make you feel good." Kin's soft voice melted Sef's hearts. Her siphon pumped with renewed vigor, speeding them toward the shipwreck they had adopted as their temporary home. She sent out a sounding pulse as they approached but hit nothing larger than a scupper. She descended to the silty bottom and crawled into the broken, barnacle-encrusted hull.

She pressed her back against the opening and hardened it, leaving one tentacle dangling outside to sense anything approaching, then spread her skirt out along the soft wood. Kin unlatched from her duct and wriggled out of her pad. He darted between her eyes and flashed a series of exploding patterns that stirred a faint spark within her.

Go ahead, she flashed, flaring her siphon and turning her body blood red. Kin flashed from red to white several times, then disappeared from her sight as he nestled into the bottom of her opening. Her gills fluttered as his tentacles traced delicate lines around her rim. His tiny cups attached and detached in rapid succession, sending tingles throughout her body, down to the tips of her tentacles.

She brought a pad in close and pressed it against the back of his head, freezing his caresses for a moment as his pleasure surged through the connection. He soon began his tender ministrations again, exploring just inside the rim of her siphon, where her skin was so thin she could feel the smooth texture of his cups, their hard edges stuttering against her membranes, flooding her with dizzying clouds of ecstasy. She felt her skin soften, and she released the pad from his head to steady herself. Kin's tentacles went limp.

Not safe to go soft here, she flashed with her pad.

Kin released from her siphon, which ached at his absence. He curled up against her pad, and their connection re-formed. He radiated understanding and a love so complete and unconditional it sent shivers across her skin. Spots of bright white sped like shooting stars across her skirt, radiating out to the tips of her tentacles, which sparkled and swayed in the buffered current. She pulled Kin in close, forming a cone with one of her tentacles and wrapping her skirt around it, leaving only a small opening at the top so she could look in on him as he slept.

He was so small, so fragile. There were a thousand different things in the bay that would eat him if given half a chance, but Sef would never let that happen. She was going to find them a new home, a safe one where dwemer flowed freely and unoccupied crevices abounded—if such a place still existed.

"It does," came Kin's sleepy voice. *"We'll find it."*

He left unsaid what would happen once they finally found a new home and settled in. Communion was a big commitment, one she'd always dreamed of. Kin was a rare pearl, clever and playful but ever deferential to her needs. There was no one she'd rather spend every waking moment with.

And yet.

The thought of merging with him filled her with melancholy dread. She would miss his flitting, his exuberant color patterns, the way he nuzzled around her cups. And while everyone said the bond after communion was so much stronger and more intimate than the courting period, she didn't want anything to change. She wanted this Kin, in this form, and she wanted her own mind to herself.

Kin stirred, pulling the corners of her pad, which had loosened as she pondered. She squeezed with gentle pressure, and Kin's peace flowed into her. They had time to figure it out, and she had time to prepare herself for the inevitable. They had lost their home, but they would find a new one. She was sure of it. Any thoughts of communion were kelp dreams anyway until they had sufficient food, shelter, and dwemer.

She coiled her protective cone a little tighter, pressing her eye against the opening, and stared down at her pad, where several of Kin's tentacles hung out like the fringe on a mussel. Her hearts grew full for this tiny, brilliant creature.

"I will always keep you safe," she said softly. Kin's cups pressed gently against hers, and she joined him in an inky black sleep.

Sef and Kin returned to the source of the dwemered water the next day. The channel it ran through was blocked by thick metal bars across the entrance, with another set of bars further in, covered in some kind of metal mesh. A smaller school of silversides made an easy snack, and Sef left one floating for Kin to peck at. He didn't need food, since her ducts had started producing at first bonding, but he enjoyed a bit of fresh flesh. His sharp little beak took chunk after tiny chunk out of the fish's soft belly. When he'd had enough, he flitted toward the screened grate and peeled away the corner of the mesh, which came off easily. He flashed excitedly. *"I can swim upstream and check it out if you want!"*

Sef flashed *NO!* so hard that Kin's tentacles sagged; he let himself drift with the current on his side, as if dead. Sef swept him up in her pad and brought him close to her eye. She could tell by the slight wiggle of his tips that he was faking, but she admired his dedication to his craft.

"I could squeeze through there myself if I wanted," she said. *"But who knows what might be lurking inside that tunnel?"*

"Love, that's where the dwemer is coming from. Our dwemer. You tasted it. You know."

Sef opened her pad. Kin hovered by her eye with gentle flips of his skirt, fixing her with a gaze made all the more intense by his tiny size. He was right, of course. Dwemer from different vents had different flavors, and none of them ever satisfied Sef as much as her home vent—until the humans had covered it with a great metal bell and pipes reaching up to the surface. Sef didn't quite understand how, but they must have found a way to harvest and store the dwemer, which they were known to use in their devices. She wondered if they even knew the diaspora they had caused.

Not now, she flashed.

"When, exactly?" Kin hovered so close to her eye she could feel the little current from his skirt flapping.

"You're not going to let this go, are you?"

"SEF, THEY TOOK OUR HOME!" Kin flashed in a spectrum of angry colors, settling on a shadowy gray with red at the tips of his tentacles and around his eyes.

Sef lowered her pad next to him, but he veered away from it, still fixing her with an angry glare. She sucked in a fresh load of dwemer-tinged water, then blew it out slowly.

"Okay, we'll come back tomorrow and take a look."

Kin's shade lightened, the red and gray giving way to purple and pink as his tentacles wriggled with excitement.

"A careful look, Kin."

"It's you who needs to be careful, love. Humans don't hunt me. They hunt you."

Kin's words echoed in her mind that night as he lay curled up in her pad. *They hunt you.* She'd seen a few common osmo picked off by spearfishers or entangled in their nets; she supposed that to humans she would appear to be just a strange osmo. In their territory, in featureless stone channels with nowhere to hide, she would be taking a risk. And to be fair, humans might reasonably see her as a threat and defend themselves accordingly. She would need to be on her best camouflage game, which would hopefully be made easier by the steady, if thin, supply of dwemer in the water flowing into the river from beyond the grate.

She wasn't quite sure what they'd do if they found the source of the dwemer. From all the evidence, the humans must be storing the dwemer somewhere nearby and distributing it to power their devices. Cutlers made it a point to know as little about humans as possible, other than the importance of avoiding them, but she was starting to regret her ignorance. One way or another, she was going to find out something, if only to soften the fire in Kin's eyes.

THREE

Seara shone her headlamp into the outflow channel, which still ran clear since the tide was low. A lone silverside held steady in the stream, keeping itself in place by waving its tail side to side.

"Fuck," Seara muttered under her breath. There must be a tear in the screen again. She unclipped the hoop net from her side, fixed it on the end of her pole, and gently lowered it into the water just downstream from the fish. She tapped her headlamp on and off repeatedly with one hand to distract the fish while bracing the pole against her other forearm. She moved the net behind it, using all the muscles in her back and leg to hold it steady against the current. Her finger slipped off the button as she tried to turn the lamp back on; by the time she found the button again, the fish had disappeared and her net was empty.

"Well, isn't that just a crusty bunghole." Her voice echoed off the walls of the channel. She sighed, unshouldered her pack, and dug out her waders. She scanned the darkness in all directions, listening for the faintest sound, but she was alone, as usual. She slipped out of her boots and pants and into her waders, securing the straps over her shoulder without unbuttoning them. They were too big for her, and the right boot had a pinhole leak, but with any luck she wouldn't be in long enough for it to matter.

She flopped over to the nearest ladder and climbed down into the water, whose warmth she could feel through the waxed canvas. The unnaturally clean smell was overwhelming up close, and she knew from experience it could make a person go loopy if they spent too much time around it. Even from above the channel, it was enough to send her home with a headache after each shift.

She saw several more silversides shimmering in the light from her headlamp. Not enough to panic, but enough to get her ass fired if she didn't do something about it. She pulled the pliers from the inside pocket of her waders as she approached the screen, where the problem was as evident as it was confounding. A corner of the screen was bent away from its moorings—not torn but peeled back.

Not by a silverside, surely, nor a trench rat or anything else she could imagine. Unless it had come from inside the plant, whatever had bent the screen must have passed through the outer gate, whose bars were a hand's width apart. As she fought to bend the screen back into place, she tried to imagine what creature besides a human could possibly do such a thing.

Seara's scream echoed off the narrow walls of the channel as a huge splash erupted and something massive and toothy slammed into the grille less than ten spans away. Seara fell backward, flooding her waders with warm discharge water. Her bladder released as the creature hurled itself against the grille again, teeth like swords clattering against the bars, its mouth nearly filling the opening. The bars held, and the creature disappeared into the suddenly frothing water outside the grate. She scrambled to her feet, almost losing her footing on the slick concrete at the bottom of the channel as she backed slowly toward the ladder, some fifty spans away. She barely stopped herself from screaming when the creature slammed into the bars again, then vanished into the muddy foam.

Seara's heart ricocheted around her ribcage as she watched the water, waiting for another explosion that never came. The creature's image was burned into her mind: great hinged jaws big enough to swallow a vendor's cart whole, with rows of glistening clear-gray teeth as long as her forearm. Beyond the mouth, the details were fuzzier, but its body was between snake and eel, a hundred times bigger and covered with bony plates on top. Seara reached the ladder but had to wait a few moments for her hands to stop shaking before she was ready to climb up to safety. It was a rough climb with her waders full, but she wasn't about to remove them in the water.

She flopped down on the stone, water from her waders sloshing under her back as she shimmied and squeaked her way free of them. She dried herself as best she could with the filthy rag in her pack, which wasn't really meant for her skin, but was all she had. She slipped her pants on over her still-damp legs and soaked underwear and sat down on a roll of mesh next to the channel.

She squeezed her hands together to stop them from shaking. She'd seen some weird shit in the Trench—dead bodies, glowing eels, even a swamp dragon longer than a man once—but what she had just seen was impossible. Maybe in the deep ocean such a monster could exist, but she'd never heard of anything like it. And in the morning, she'd be out in the flats in a small boat like bait.

"I'm home, Da."

He was hunched on the couch, staring at his Fascinator, which was beginning to dim. She'd need to get a new reservoir after her game warden shift.

"Da?"

He raised his eyebrows, but his gaze remained fixed on the orb. Its glow cycled from purple through a rainbow of colors, ending in red before going dark for a moment and starting again at purple. Seara sat down next to him, put her hand on his knee, and watched the lights of the globe reflected on her father's wrinkled face. Each time the globe went to purple, his face fell, then lifted little by little as it cycled toward red. She knew the pattern by heart, could see the colors in her sleep. It was oddly relaxing after a long day, and her legs were spent from all the standing and wading and climbing. She sat watching it with him for way too long before she finally pushed off his leg and lifted her tired, creaky body off the couch.

She made herself eat leftover, slightly crusty pasta, then boiled some water and made a fresh batch for Da. He fed himself with slow, trembling movements, never taking his eyes off the globe. Without it, she'd have to feed him every bite, which was not how she preferred to spend her few waking moments at home.

"I saw something strange at the plant today."

Da's brows lifted and stayed up. He was listening.

"You're probably going to think I'm making this up. You always said I had an overactive imagination."

He blinked, and a faint smile formed on his lips.

"You remember those gnasher eels we used to catch at night from the public docks?"

His body twitched with a hint of laughter.

"Well, imagine one fifty spans long with a mouth big enough to swallow this couch."

Da's eyes drifted from the globe toward her, meeting her gaze with his own unsteady, watery one.

"Seara," he croaked, beckoning her over. "My girl."

She scooched closer and put her hand on his shoulder.

"I'm here, Da. I'm right here."

His eyes slowly peeled from hers, and his face returned to its usual blank state as he stared at the globe's ever-changing colors. She sat with him for a little while, until her eyes stung whenever she blinked, and she nearly fell asleep sitting up.

"Let me help you to the washroom before bed."

Da let her pull him to standing and walk him to the facilities. She set the globe on the little stand facing the toilet and closed the door, leaning against it for physical and moral support. The thought of her bed made her ache for sleep, but she managed to stay upright long enough to help him back to the couch and tuck him in.

"Goodnight, Da. I'll be up early on the boat. Mr. Joven will bring you some flat rolls and tea."

"Tea," he murmured. The orb cast an eerie blue tint over his drooping eyelids, his sunken cheeks, his now drooling mouth.

Seara just made it to bed before she passed out. She woke what felt like moments later to the first gray hint of dawn filtering in through the lone window. The faint light from the orb down the hall painted the ceiling with moving colors. She fell asleep watching them and woke again to the unmistakable glare of the morning sun. She rubbed her eyes, calculating the time it would take her to dress Da, make herself some tea, and scarf down a stale cheese roll from the day before. She swung her legs off the bed with a groan.

Time to do it all over again.

Seara's waxed coat and hat kept the drizzle at bay, but chilly drops found their way to her skin here and there. Between that and the random bursts of wind, she was depressingly cold, and it was hard to do much about it on the boat. Ray pulled up the oars once they entered the seathorn flats, and they poled their way through with deliberate, quiet movements so as not to startle their quarry.

Fishing in the flats was against the law, since so many species used it as a nursery and their populations were already stressed by pollution and overfishing elsewhere. Seara and Ray were as close to the law as could be found offshore, but they carried no weapons, unless belt knives and catchpoles counted. The trophy hunters they were after would have powered nets and harpoons, along with the latest dwemer slings. While they weren't likely to shoot a warden, they were so used to doing what they wanted with impunity that Seara's stomach always churned at first contact.

Seara saw it in the distance between clumps of seathorn, a low-slung platform boat with a dwemer pump engine that could shoot it out of range in a matter of seconds. She slowed the boat with her pole, making the agreed-upon *tssk* sound to let Ray know she'd spotted them. They came to a stop without making any ripples. Seara wedged her pole in the seathorn roots and secured it in the holder. She uncapped her field scope and studied the trophy boat.

Two men with new sharkskin jackets stood on opposite corners of the platform with their hands on the grips of harpoons in dwemer slings, scanning the water intently. A third man slouched on a stool, one hand on the wheel and the other fiddling with something in his fingers. The boat was angled facing her, so she couldn't see the registration number painted on the side.

Seara picked up her pole and used her eyes to tell Ray to do the same. If they moved slowly, using the seathorn for cover, they might get close enough to identify the boat so even if the hunters fled, she could track them down at the docks. They poled their way into the narrow passage between two long stands of seathorn and were about to slip noiselessly behind the next piece of cover when a pair of painted ducks took off squawkily, drawing the attention of the hunters. Seara froze, hoping the camouflage patterns on the boat and her raincoat would work miracles, but it was not to be. The men exchanged a few tense words, then the driver straightened up and pulled a lever. The boat sped off with a gushing noise that was loud even from this distance, spewing up enough spray in its wake that she couldn't make out the markings.

"Well, fuck me with a rusty gaff." Seara maneuvered her pole into the holder again and leaned her head against it, staring down into the greenish water between the brown masses of seathorn roots. Her body hair rose in unison as a section of the roots detached from the rest and hovered just a few spans below the surface. The roots rippled in the current, then unfurled with sinuous grace, spreading wide like a parasol, then began glowing green and gold in a slow pattern like her father's orb. Seara relaxed at once, even as a long green tentacle with a small paddle-shaped end snaked out of the water. She knew she should be afraid, possibly even doubting her sanity, but she felt only curiosity and wonder as it seemed to study her for a moment, then slid back into the water without making a splash.

Ray's face had paled to the color of ripe wheat. He gripped the gunwale as he wheezed for breath. His eyes had the glassy, faraway look Seara knew all too well. She reached into his pocket, found his breather, and stuck it in his mouth. His eyes fluttered closed, then opened again. His hand soon found the breather, and she moved hers to his shoulder. He blinked thanks, took one more deep breath, then tucked the breather back in his pocket.

"What...the brine-encrusted...fuck...was that?" he croaked between shallow breaths.

"Some kind of osmo, I think, but..." Seara trailed off as she pictured the leaf-shaped pad it had stuck out of the water. It might have been a sensory organ, but she'd never heard of an osmo with anything like it.

"When it came up, I..." Ray's breathing had evened out, but his eyes remained troubled. "Did you feel something?"

Seara pursed her lips. Ray was given to flights of fancy, and she didn't want to encourage him, but she *had* felt something, hadn't she? That sense of calm that swept away her fear couldn't have been natural. The thing's body was half the size of their boat, and with the tentacles it was even longer. She should have been shitting her pants, but instead she'd only been curious.

"I don't know, Ray. What did you feel?"

Ray studied the water, where the seathorn swayed in the current.

"I felt like..." He pulled a toothpick out of his pocket and tucked it in the corner of his mouth. "I felt calm, like it wasn't a threat. Like it didn't see us as a threat." He shook his head. "Didn't stop it from triggering my wheeze though."

"I guess we can both add 'making friends with strange osmo' to our resumés. In the meantime, we need to check out the lower flats before the tide changes."

Ray nodded, absently unhooking his pole from the holder.

They saw another hunter boat speeding off as they approached the lower flats, but it was too far away and too fast for them to catch its numbers. It was pointless anyway; the fine for illegal hunting was only a hundred marks, and a boat like that used twice as much in dwemer every trip. No wonder the price kept rising. She sighed as she remembered she had to get a new reservoir for Da's globe on the way home; she only had four bells between shifts as it was. She was going to be dead on her feet at the plant tonight. But what else was new?

She bumped fists with Ray as he tied up the boat, then made her way through the steady drizzle to the dwemer shop closest to her apartment. She paid fifty marks for the reservoir, which would have cost forty only a year ago, though she'd get back ten for the deposit whenever she had time to swap the old one out. She could've gotten one for forty if she'd been willing to walk to the lower city, but time was as much the enemy as money.

These days, both were; Da's pension had been decimated during the last government finance debacle. Even working two jobs, she could barely afford rent, food, and dwemer. If prices kept rising, she was going to find herself living in the lower city. Without at least a downtown address, her chances of getting accepted into the nursing program at Umian Public were even closer to zero. Of course, if she didn't finish her last two correspondence courses by the end of the year, that was all moot anyway.

Da's clothes were wet, as was the towel on the couch beneath him. His rheumy eyes were apologetic as he glanced up from the globe, which glowed dimly with its almost empty reservoir. Seara closed her eyes, pressing her hand to her forehead in the hope of stopping her tears, but they spilled hot down her face.

"Don't cry, my little otter." Da's voice had the exact same cadence as in the old days when he said phrases like that. Fresh tears immediately replaced the ones she wiped away.

"It's fine, Da. Let's get you to the washroom to change."

"I couldn't..." Da's brow furrowed as he stared at the dimming globe. "I forgot."

"Well, I got you a new reservoir, so your globe will be nice and shiny once we've got you into some dry clothes."

"Shiny?" he asked in a small, hopeful voice, looking up from the globe for a moment.

"Like the sun, Da. *After* we get you cleaned up."

"Shiny," he cooed, accepting her hand and shuffling along toward the washroom with her.

By the time she'd changed him, laid out a dry towel, changed the reservoir, and fed them both seabiscuits and tea, Seara was too tired to make it to her bed. She passed out on the couch with the ever-changing lights of the globe painting her eyelids. One more shift at the plant and she had half a day off. She would sleep, do a little shopping, make some soup for the week, and work on her chemistry homework at the Hilltop library. And maybe while she was there, she'd have time to look up the menagerie of monsters that seemed to be popping up everywhere she went.

And then four days of double shifts in a row.

She wasn't made for this shit.

No one was made for this shit. This wasn't a life; it was systemic abuse, and the only way out was to cling to the hems of the abusers.

Just as the rage threatened to rip her from sleep altogether, her mind flashed with the peace she'd felt when the creature had flashed its soft green pattern. She exhaled deeply as sleep pulled her into its dark, velvety folds.

FOUR

Kin lay nestled in Sef's pad, watching her colors ripple as she slept, like sunlight filtering through waves. She was as beautiful in sleep as she was awake, but her colors were muted these days with the daily struggle for dwemer. He longed to see her in her full glory again, as she was when they first met. He'd zipped over the top of a coral ridge chasing a wounded silverside, and the ridge had risen to encircle him like a bowl. His hearts had skipped a beat until he realized she was a cuttler, not an osmo, and she wasn't trying to eat him; she was courting him. He'd flitted around and around, pretending to try to escape, and she'd gently nudged him back down again and again.

She was so gorgeous, long and flowy and elegant; how could she have any interest in a runt like him? He'd often dreamt of being a proper cuttler, beautiful and deadly as the sea itself, queen of her many-splendored realm. Being surrounded by Sef's bulk, warmed with her gentle touches and gentler thoughts, was the closest he'd ever felt to that dream. He knew from that moment that whatever it took, if she would have him, he would cleave to her for all time. If he couldn't become one with her, if he couldn't *become* her, there was no reason to go on.

Sef blended to brownish gray and her tentacles stopped twitching as she cycled into quiet sleep. Kin was wide awake and feeling peckish; he eyed her ducts but didn't want to disturb her. He released gently and pulsed up out of the cone of her coiled tentacle. A pair of lesser violets nipped at the algae growing in a crack between the boards of the shipwreck, turning sideways to fix him with their big, round eyes. He let himself spread out and float, turning green and taking on the texture of a stray leaf of sea oats. He drifted toward them with gentle pulses, as if moved by current. One of the violets swam closer with a flicker of its fins, then stopped just out of reach, angling this way and that to determine what he was. He drifted closer; the fish darted in to nip at one of his tentacles, the last mistake it would ever make. Kin snatched it up, delivering a quick bite to the brain to end its life, and the other violet disappeared through the crack.

He sucked out the eyes, his favorite part, so unctuous and satisfying, then tore open its belly with his beak and picked out the choicest organs, though the fish here had little dwemer and could only nourish his muscles. He didn't want to fill up, since Sef would awaken soon. His morning feed was an important part of their bonding and the most pleasurable moment of his day. Sef stirred, uncoiling her tentacles and flaring danger yellow for a moment until she saw him and relaxed into a chiding orange.

Don't do that to me, she flashed.

"I was hungry, and you're so beautiful when you sleep."

Sef deepened to a dark red, and her pad swept him out of the water and brought him in close to her big golden eye.

"Come, let's get you fed."

Her pad settled down in the folds of her skirt, and her ducts swelled as he massaged them with his tentacles. He pulled one open with his cups as his feeding tube extended, swelling to form a perfect seal. He narrowed his pupils as the dwemer flowed in, strong and hot. He worried that she might be expending too much on him, but the flood of ecstasy soon erased all thoughts. His skirt clung to her pad, pulling trickles from her other ducts, which half-opened with the suction.

Her pleasure thrummed into him as her pad went taut and a kaleidoscope of colors flashed through his mind. She filled him to overflowing, and his ink released in a moment of transcendent bliss. Her body tensed, then relaxed, and her duct closed as Kin's tube slowly retracted. He caressed her with the backsides of his tentacles as her colors faded from crimson to violet to blue before settling to brownish-gray once again.

Mmmmmm, Kin flashed. *"You taste so good. I hope you're not giving me too much."*

"I'll keep feeding you until the very last drop is spent."

Kin felt his body flushing sad blue, and he perked it back up to pink as he pulsed toward one of her golden eyes.

"We'll find another dwemer source together, my love. And when we do…" He did not say the words, but she blinked her understanding. They were so close already; once they found a new vent, they could complete their bonding and be together, body and mind, until the end of their days. Kin could shed his stubby form and be big and flowy and beautiful with her, as he was always meant to be.

Kin stayed in Sef's skirt as they traveled up the channel into the human city. When Sef finally slowed and opened up, he swam out into the pocket of clear, dwemer-laced water flowing from behind the metal bars. The human with the dwemer net was nowhere to be seen.

"I'm still not comfortable with you going in there alone." Sef's body had flushed to deep purple with warning yellow on the tips of her tentacles.

"And I'm still not comfortable not knowing what the source of this dwemer is." In truth, he was curious about more than that; he'd always been fascinated by tales of humans and their cities, like great dryland reefs.

Sef blinked slowly, flaring her siphon, then went black.

"I'll wait right here, but if you're not back soon, I'm coming after you."

Kin nuzzled her forehead, then flipped around and flared his skirt a few times before darting between the bars and into the clearwater channel. He swam up to the second set of bars, the one with the thin metal screen, which someone had repaired since his last visit. It didn't take much to peel it back again, and he reminded himself to return it to its former shape when he left so as not to arouse suspicion. He wasn't sure how clever humans were, but no sense leaving evidence of his passage.

The water was warm, clean, just saline enough, and suffused with faint dwemer, giving a little pep to his pulses. He swam in short bursts, scanning the area ahead for unusual shapes or movement as he went. The barrier had done a good job of keeping fish out; not even a single silverside was to be seen. Other than some unusually lush moss, the channel was bare stone, the kind humans fabricated out of sand, pebbles, and minerals. They were even more efficient than coral when it came to building their habitats; beyond the walls of the channel, Kin saw blocks and columns of fabricated stone with an assortment of mostly rectangular features. His stomach tingled at the realization that he was in the human city now, all alone. He hadn't been this far away from Sef since the humans had capped the vent back home. She had always been overprotective of him, which was kind of sweet; he could take care of himself, though he sometimes wondered if Sef really understood that.

A pair of oblong creatures with thin tails scurried along the edge of the wall, staring down into the water every so often. They weren't much bigger than Kin, and when they stopped and peered down into the water near him, he flashed a brief fascination pattern, then went dark. The creatures stared at him, though he doubted they could see him against the stone of the channel in the dim light of evening. They turned toward each other, then stared back down, and he flashed the pattern again, letting it play out for a moment. They sat entranced, unmoving, as any aquatic creature would, until he let the pattern fade. It made sense; the humans in the boat had responded to Sef's tranquility pattern. However different they might be, these creatures' visual intelligence should be responsive to his abilities. He hoped he didn't have to test it further. He swam on, and the creatures continued their way along the wall.

The channel bent one way, then another, passing through a series of irregular spaces above before becoming a squared tunnel with faint light from beyond. The water grew warmer, and the dwemer was a little stronger here; some of it must have evaporated into the air as it flowed toward the river. It was a bit like approaching his vent from far away; he could taste it, sense it in his blood, but it wasn't home.

He came to another set of bars covered in mesh like the one he'd crossed through before. By now, the tunnel glowed with unnatural yellow light from where it opened into an enormous pool ahead. He plastered himself against the wall, adjusting his color and texture to match it, and studied the area. Clear water flowed into the reservoir from another opening in the opposite wall, with a gate to match the one he clung to. They must have filtered the river water somehow before it arrived here. The water was quite warm, almost uncomfortably so. The source of the heat was immediately apparent.

Two huge cylindrical structures of metal and glass straddled the edge of the reservoir, each as big around as the hull of a ship. The blue tint of the dwemer behind the glass appeared almost green beneath bright yellow lights fixed in the ceiling. The lights were dwemer-powered, which made sense; cuttlers and other creatures near the vent used dwemer to shine lights for luring or blinding prey or warding off predators. The humans were known to use it to fuel their boats and weapons, and the huge metal constructs they'd used to cap the vent must have been dwemer-powered somehow.

Several humans patrolled a ledge that ran around the periphery of the space, shining lights into the water as they went. Kin edged closer, flitting to press himself against the mesh blocking access to the main pool. One of the humans above shone their light down in the water, and he froze, hoping his camouflage was good enough.

After the humans flashed their lights around for a moment longer, one of them waved to another, who approached holding a thin, rectangular object in their hands. Kin didn't stick around to find out what it was. He let go and drifted, changing to greenish gray to match the channel, and was soon safely out of sight. As he floated down the artificial stone chute, the vision of those towers full of dwemer dominated his thoughts.

That was home. Not only could he taste it in the water; he could feel it in his guts, the way he could tell Sef was angry long before she changed colors. The way a ravager's approach triggered something deep inside. The way he warmed returning to the reef after a sojourn away.

That life was gone now. The dwemer from their reef, their home, filled tanks in the human city. They used it for their lights, their boats, and Depths knew what else. It was a resource to be extracted and consumed in an endless cycle until there was none left. If there was anything humans were known for, it was exhausting nature's bounty, then finding new ways to exploit it, new realms to conquer and despoil. Disposable magic.

What could a tiny cuttler do about a problem so vast? Sef with her great size and strong tentacles could at least fight, though he wasn't sure what good one cuttler could do. But all he knew how to do was love her and try to survive long enough to join with her. If they could ever find a new reef, another vent somewhere that wasn't already overcrowded with refugees.

He let himself roll upside down with the current, watching the screen get closer and closer until it caught him. He melded to its shape and color, a game he sometimes played with Sef, to see if he could sneak up on her. She could sense his presence just as he could hers, but he could sometimes fool her eyes.

He crept along the screen toward the opening he'd made, then slipped through and folded it closed. The size of the screens would keep out any but the smallest fish, and the humans had repaired the tear within the day. Maybe the fish caused problems with their dwemer machine. He clung to the wall for a moment, studying the last bit of channel ahead and the clear patch where it entered the river.

Sef wasn't there. Neither was the warm net of her mind, which he should have been able to sense by now. Something was wrong. He darted forward, sticking close to the wall, and paused at the edge. He narrowed his pupils and focused his mind, searching for Sef. Her signature was nowhere to be found; only a few eels and a turtle, and something big, maybe a mouthfish—no, this was bigger than that. He knew this energy, this angry hunger that could never be sated. It was impossible, here in this narrow canal in the human city—

Kin shaped and colored himself like a barnacle as the oversized head came into view, twice as big around as Sef, mouth filled with clear-gray teeth. The beast's head wiggled side to side with the movement of its long, sinuous body. It stopped, turning a big silvery eye toward the outflow. Toward Kin.

He dared not move a tentacle. A creature of this size probably wouldn't bother with something as small as him, but ravagers had a special hatred of cuttlers, which was more than reciprocated. It cocked its head this way and that, then swiveled back toward the canal and continued upstream. Its body seemed to go on forever, easily five times as long as Sef. *Sef.*

Where was Sef?

He inched toward the edge of the canal, watching the ravager's tail disappear into the muddy water. He felt her then, a gentle tug, the kind that didn't travel far; ravagers were thought to be sensitive to the cuttlers' communication waves, though it was doubtful they understood them. This advantage made them the only predator that regularly fed on his kind. One that until now was never known to stray from deep waters.

"Quickly," Sef said. *"Just downstream."*

He saw her then, flattened against the muddy bottom just below the outflow. He zipped down, following the contours of her body until he found her skirt and slipped inside.

"That was close," she said as she detached from the bottom and began to float downstream.

"I guess we aren't the only ones whose homes the humans stole."

Sef did not respond, but her mood was sour as she swam out of the narrow canal and into the river mouth's labyrinth of obstacles and currents. She relaxed somewhat as they dropped below the shelf and into the depths where their shipwreck awaited, their hole unoccupied. Sef had swiped it with her musk, which only other cuttlers could sense, to claim it as theirs. Kin's hearts warmed as the familiar scent flooded his gills. Home. It smelled like home.

Sef pressed her back against the hole in the hull and unfurled her skirt. Kin darted out and turned to face her. She tinted herself deep green with soft blue spots, meaning she wanted to talk. Kin mimicked her colors in reverse, getting the expected pink bloom between her eyes.

Cutie, she flashed.

"*Beauty*," he answered. Her pink bloom took a turn toward red, then faded as her pupils narrowed on him.

"*Enough with the flattery. Tell me what you saw.*"

Five

Cliff handed the receptionist his battered library card. His research privileges had expired two years ago when he'd failed to complete the free correspondence course he'd enrolled in, but the date was hard to read.

"This card's seen some good use," she commented, squinting to read it.

"I've been meaning to get it replaced, but..." He flashed his gentlest smile. She was an uptowner with a downtown accent. One of the lucky ones who'd made it out. He'd worn his 'clean' clothes, meaning they'd been washed in the Trench at high tide and dried in the breeze long enough to take most of the stink out of them, but no one would mistake him for an uptowner.

"I can do that for you right now if you like." She pulled out a card and a pen and started writing before Cliff knew what was happening. "I can't quite read the date on the research privileges, so we'll just set it until, say, two years from today?"

Cliff's mouth hung open for a moment before he stammered, "S-sure, yeah, that sounds about right."

She winked and continued filling out the card, mouth working over a spiceball. Cliff used to love those as a kid. The one woman he'd kissed—or rather, who'd kissed him—had spiceball breath, which he'd enjoyed more than the kiss. Not that there was anything wrong with it, or with her; he just didn't—

"Here you..." The clerk pulled out a stamp and pounded a green circle with the Hilltop library insignia in the middle of his card. "Go!"

"Thank you so much," he said, fingering the fresh card, the sharp corners.

"That's why I'm here! Anything else?"

Cliff tapped the card. It had been a while since he'd been here, and he'd never set foot in the science wing. "I'm looking for information on sea creatures. Cephalopods, to be exact. I was hoping there'd be some kind of illustrated guide or something."

She raised her eyebrows conspiratorially. "Is this because of the new *Savage Adventures*?"

"No, I—what? The new one has a..."

She nodded, looking pleased with herself. "All ten copies are checked out. It has a tentacle romance that I hear is *quite* juicy. I can put you on the waitlist if you want."

"Yeah, that'd be great actually, thank you!" He went to hand her his card, but she was already writing in her ledger.

"Check back in three days. We get pretty quick turnaround on those."

"Thank you, I will."

"And the life sciences books are on the second floor, south wing." She pointed her pen at a map affixed to the wall, then wrote a title and reference number on a slip of paper. "This one's popular." He slowly remembered the layout of the library as he studied the map.

"Okay, great." He tapped the paper against his hand. "Thank you. Thank you so much."

"Happy hunting, Mr. Hennis."

The slot where the book should have been was empty. He checked the number the clerk had written down and looked up and down the shelf in case it had been mis-shelved, to no avail. He leafed through a few other books that looked similar, but none of them had anything about an osmo with two tentacles on the front. He was wandering around the stacks, looking for inspiration, when he saw a woman seated at a table studying a book open to a two-page illustration of an osmo.

She had orange-brown skin and plenty of wrinkles for her age, which he took to be about forty. Then again, who didn't have extra wrinkles these days? Cliff avoided mirrors like a vampire. She wore a uniform, security guard, maybe; the line down the sleeves and pants almost made him flinch. He'd seldom had a positive experience with anyone in a uniform.

Her face was sad but kind, like she was doing her best despite it all. She was a downtowner, he guessed from the wear on her shoes. She had access to the university library; she must be either a student or an instructor. It could be a coincidence that they were both looking for *Legends of the Deep Revealed*, but to have the book open to that page—

"Something I can help you with?" Her tone was sharp but polite, the kind that said 'Stay the fuck away from me, trench rat.' He almost turned and fled out of sheer embarrassment, but her expression eased as she watched him. "Sorry, I didn't mean—"

"You're fine," he said softly, moving closer to get a better look at the book while keeping enough distance to make her feel safe. "It seems we have similar taste in literature." He gestured toward the book, which she covered with her hands for a moment. She relaxed, turning toward him and sighing a smile.

"I'm Seara." She held out her fist, and he leaned forward to tap it with his. "You got a thing for osmo?"

She pushed out the chair next to her, and Cliff sat gingerly, staring at the creature on the pages.

"Only recently, though they're magnificent creatures, if the pictures tell the truth." The osmo depicted was red on its oblong head, which protruded from the water next to a rowboat about as long as the creature. A dozen purple tentacles with pink suction cups trailed below the surface, several coiled tight around fish or crustaceans. Its big eyes stared at a terrified man holding the oars; the illustration even depicted the sweat running down his face.

"Recently?" she asked with a slight quaver in her voice. When he met her eyes, he saw fear and wonder in equal measure. He nodded, glancing down at the book.

"The Channel Osmo is thought to measure up to fifteen spans from crown to tip," he read aloud, almost to himself. That was more than twice as long as a person was tall. He read on in silence. *Little is known about their behavior, but multiple sources have described the creatures as curious, even playful, around humans.*

"That's not even the biggest one." Seara flipped a few pages back, where a fold-out illustration showed a charcoal-gray osmo wrapping its tentacles around a ship. "It says these are thought to be extinct, though."

"Thank the clouds for small favors."

Seara sucked her teeth. "I'd love to have seen one. To think that such creatures existed, only to be…" She trailed off, running her fingers lightly over the page.

"We do have a way of destroying the world's wonders," Cliff murmured.

"Not all of them." She flipped forward past the Channel Osmo and a handful of others, each more unusually shaped than the last. Cliff stifled a gasp as she stopped on a page showing two osmo, one huge and deep blue with yellow spots, the other tiny and pink, less than a hundredth of its partner's size. The larger one held out two tentacles with pads on the ends, with a series of faint colored lines between the two creatures, like what comics used to depict telepathy. If these weren't the creatures he'd seen in the Trench, they were awfully close. The page was titled *Reef Dazzlers.*

Reef Dazzlers are among the most elusive of osmo, able to change color in an instant and swim faster than any daggerfish. But what makes these creatures truly unique is an apparent ability to use auto-generated dwemer waves to communicate, defend themselves, and even attack. Isolated reports tell of an ability to hypnotize and calm humans, and possibly even communicate with them, presumably using the same waves. Scientific efforts to study this phenomenon have thus far remained unsuccessful.

"That's it," Seara breathed, staring at the page as if in disbelief. Cliff's head buzzed with the implications. Had she seen it too? Had the creatures he'd seen by the outflow from the power plant hypnotized him? Or were they trying to communicate?

"What about its teeth?" Cliff scanned the page until he found it.

Dazzlers use dwemer waves to stun prey fish, then use their skirts to funnel them into their mouths, which crush them with hundreds of tiny teeth.

"That's a bit different from an osmo," Seara said. "They catch prey with their tentacles and deliver it to mouths with raspy-toothed tongues."

"Are you a life scientist?"

She quirked a half smile. "Trying to be. It's hard, with..." She gestured at her uniform.

"I feel you." Cliff felt guilty at first; he didn't have a job. He was just a skimmer. He mind-kicked himself; skimmers like him caught the waste the power plant put out, saved it from flowing out into the sea. Kept the cost low, too; most shops downtown bought their cells from the recharge at a steep discount. It was the same dwemer; why pay double for it uptown?

"Speaking of which, I have to go to work." She closed the book and picked it up apologetically. "I'll have it back within a week."

"Okay," was all Cliff managed as she stood to leave. She was the one person he could talk to about what he'd seen; he couldn't just let her go like that.

"It was nice to meet you, Cliff." She blinked and smiled, turning to go.

"Have you seen it?" he whispered, loud enough for her to hear. She stopped and stood still for a long moment, then turned around, studying his face, his eyes. She gave an almost imperceptible nod.

"Out in the flats."

"What were you doing in the flats? Fishing?" He cursed his foolish tongue, but she smiled.

"I work for the conservancy, protecting the osmo from hunters." Her face fell for a moment. "Not that it does much good."

"No, that's important. People underestimate the value of the urban ecosystem."

Her smile returned, then fell again as she checked the clock on the wall. "Listen, I *really* have to go or I'll be late for my other job. Meet me here tomorrow, same time. I'll bring it back and we can talk about it."

"Oh." Cliff was too stunned to say more at first. "Sure, yeah, yes, that would be...that would be amazing."

She quirked a smile, then turned and hurried away.

"Well, I'll be," he said to himself.

Cliff sat in his tent with a day-old sausage roll and a cup of lukewarm tea, listening to the drizzle on the tarp. The dazzler couldn't have been responsible for the attack on Louie. It could certainly kill a person if it took a mind to, but not in a way that would leave sprays of blood on the ceiling above. Cliff had seen the bloodstains himself when they were still fresh. It hadn't acted like a killer; the little one had even seemed curious about him.

The more he thought about it, the more he was sure they'd tried to communicate with him. If he hadn't been so busy nearly pissing his pants, he might have been able to figure out what they were saying. There was intelligence behind those golden eyes, maybe more than a person's, even. But what were they doing in the Trench?

He packed up his skimming gear in the big duffel bag that was almost more holes than canvas at this point. He should try to scrounge one up at the Works House, but he couldn't bring himself to let something go unless he'd gotten every moment of use out of it. He carried his fishing pole, which was flimsy cover but at least gave him a pretext for being that close to the water. It wasn't illegal to fish in the Trench, though it should have been. Plenty of people ate the fish that swam in its polluted waters, one of many reasons life expectancy in the lower city was almost two decades less than uptown.

He filled half a tank in a quarter bell at the first outflow before he had to scram, then took almost until dark filling it the rest of the way below the second outflow, where the dwemer was less concentrated. He saw a couple other skimmers, whom he greeted with knowing nods. He gave them their space and didn't skim directly upstream from them. Skimmers had a code, enforced by all, which worked pretty well. They whistled when the constables approached and shared info on which recharges were buying and at what price, though you had to take skimmers' word with a pinch of salt. They were in competition, after all.

It was dark by the time he got paid and picked up another sausage roll for dinner—gods, he needed to eat vegetarian more often, but they were so cheap, and they filled him up better than the veggie ones. Skimmers couldn't be choosers.

He finished the stub of his cheroot, staring out into the churning waters where the Trench met the bay, the stink of industry and human waste all but washed away by the smoke and the briny breeze. What had this place been like a thousand years ago, before somebody decided it would make a good place for a settlement? It was tragic, what they'd done to it, but the sea was a powerful beast. There was life in the old girl yet.

In the dark of his tent, his thoughts drifted back to the creatures he'd seen. Were they really the ones from that book? And would this Seara woman actually return tomorrow as she'd promised? He hadn't told her he'd seen them, but she knew. She had to know. That was why she wanted to meet up again the next day. Wasn't it?

If he were a normal person and not a skimmer living in a tent in the lower city, he might think she was interested in him. Setting aside the absurdity of the proposition, he truly had no idea; he'd always been blind to such things until it was too late. He'd had to squirm away from a few awkward encounters in his life, though not so much since he'd lost his spot in the tiny apartment downtown he'd shared with two other skimmers. He lived alone and liked it that way.

Seara was nice, though. And smart. What had she said? That she was "trying to be" a life scientist. So, she was a student, working two jobs to make rent and pay uni fees. The power plant was supposed to pay well, and the conservancy was municipal, so it couldn't be too bad. Enough for a roof, anyway. Did she have a kid? She did have that tired look you saw on parents sometimes. But most working folk had that look these days, if not much worse.

He kept coming back to what the book had said about the dazzlers' dwemer waves. A creature like that would need a steady supply of dwemer, unless they could make their own somehow. That meant either collecting it from storms like the storm shamans he'd once dreamt of joining, or more likely from the dwemer vents found in deepwater reefs. That was where most of the dwemer in the power plant came from; vent capping had outstripped lightning rods a decade ago, leaving the storm shamans in the dustbin of history.

The only shamans to be found nowadays made their living taking uptowners on storm tours at sea. Collecting dwemer the old-fashioned way simply wasn't cost-effective anymore. Neither was skimming, but it was almost enough if you didn't have rent to pay or dependents to support.

Cliff would have given anything to be an osmo or a dazzler, swimming the ocean without such cares to weigh him down. Then again, if the dazzlers were in the city now, there had to be a reason, almost certainly not a good one. They no doubt has just as many cares as he.

SIX

Seara studied the book in the ever-changing glow of Da's Fascinator. There were a handful of other unusual osmo she hadn't heard of, but the Reef Dazzler seemed to be in a class by itself. Perhaps the most fascinating aspect was the size difference between the female and the male of the species.

The dazzler's reproductive habits are unknown, but scientists believe that the smaller creatures often seen accompanying them, less than one one-hundredth their size, are in fact the males of the species.

She smiled at the thought of a tiny man she could put in her pocket and bring out whenever she needed a fix. Not that she had much energy for that these days, or a place to bring a man even if she found one interested in a haggard forty-two-year-old who worked two jobs in polluted environments.

"Red," Da said quietly as the globe filled the room with crimson light. His favorite color. His face always fell a bit when the red faded and was replaced by purple. Then blue, then green, then yellow, then orange, then back to red. She leaned against him, staring at the red light for a moment until it changed. If he noticed her touch, he gave no sign of it.

She leaned back on the couch, studying the index for sea snakes and congrids. As much as the dazzler fascinated her, the monstrous creature she'd seen slam into the grate had her more than a little worried. Something that size could capsize the flimsy boat they used to chase osmo hunters, and its mouth was big enough to swallow a person whole. She'd never heard of anything that big in the bay, let alone the Trench. Something had to be driving these creatures to the city. She found fantastical depictions of sea serpents wrapped around ships or dragging swimmers to their deaths, but the author gave little credence to these stories. One footnote, however, gave her pause.

The largest recorded sea serpent was sixty spans long, caught by a deep-sea fishing boat that almost capsized with its weight. The creature was said to have teeth two spans long and armored plates on its back like a swamp dragon. It was too heavy to bring back to port, and a swarm of daggerfish began feasting on its living body almost immediately, so the fishermen cut the net and returned with only this unverifiable story. Based on the description, it seems more likely to be some species of giant congrid than a snake, but no other specimens have ever been observed.

"I saw a great levvie once," Da said, glancing down at her book. "Spouting in the bay. Bigger than that I bet."

Seara's eyes filled with sudden tears at hearing his voice, so much like he used to be. "I hope to see one someday."

He waved off the thought, turning back to the orb, which was orange now, inching toward his beloved red. "No levvies close to shore anymore. All gone. All gone." His face fell back to its habitual listless expression, then lifted again as the globe glowed brilliant red. He smiled, elbowing her gently.

"Red," he murmured. "So pretty."

"It sure is, Da."

Seara was dead on her feet at the power plant the next day. Nothing much happened, which made the shift drag on and on. There were no giant congrids, no dazzlers, not even a single silverside. Just leagues of walking up and down concrete paths in her broken-down shoes. She was halfway home before she remembered she was supposed to meet Cliff at Hilltop library. She trudged through the mist-dampened streets, hungry and bone-weary, but at least she didn't have to work again until midnight. She should be able to get a few good bells of sleep after dinner if Da hadn't made a mess of the place.

Cliff sat at the same table where they'd met before, reading what looked like an old issue of *Savage Adventures* with a wry smile on his face. He closed the book and slid it out of the way as if embarrassed when she pulled out a chair and sat down.

"I used to love those when I was in school." She hoped that hadn't come off as condescending, but Cliff's smile in response was genuine.

"Sometimes you just need to visit another world for a while to forget about the travails of this one."

"You got that right." She opened her bag, flicking the sheen of mist from the waxed canvas flap, and pulled the book out carefully. "I've heard it said that the deep sea is more different from our world than what you read in those books."

"The dazzler's abilities prove that theory." Cliff opened the book with a delicate touch, finding the page and studying it. "Though I can't help but wonder what a pair of them was doing in the Trench the day before yesterday." He spoke quietly, still staring at the book. She'd been pretty sure from their conversation the previous day that he'd seen one, but a pair? She wished she'd been more attentive to the one she'd seen out on the boat. Maybe the male was lurking somewhere nearby and she just hadn't noticed it.

"Where did you see them, exactly?" Most people didn't get close enough to the Trench to notice something like that, except fishermen, junkers, skimmers, and the like.

He looked up now, studying her, as if to assess whether she thought he was crazy. "Just below the outflow from the power plant." He sat back, running a hand down his weary face, scratching his scraggly beard. "I was—" He stopped, blinking a couple of times, and shook his head. "Sorry, the uniform's throwing me. I noticed the Stormchain logo on your pocket."

Seara glanced down at the logo, two intersecting infinity loops, one red, one blue. "Look, I only work when they pay me to work. And I don't give a trench rat's mange what you were doing there. I just..." She sighed through her nose, checking around for other patrons, but the life sciences wing was as empty as a graveyard. "I told you I saw one the other day, out in the flats. We were spying on an osmo hunting boat, one of those big ones with the dwemer pump engines?" Cliff closed his eyes and nodded. "We were anchored in the seathorn, waiting until the boat turned sideways so we could see the license. They saw us and sped off, and when I looked down into the water, a big patch of seathorn detached from the rest and started moving." She told him the rest of the story, leaving out no detail, so he'd feel comfortable sharing his own tale. He nodded along, listening intently, tapping the table with his fingertips when she was done.

"I was skimming dwemer," he said in a voice barely above a whisper. "It's the only work I can get these days, and it pays...well, more than nothing." He shrugged apologetically.

"No harm in that. It'd be a pity to see it go to waste, after all."

"Exactly." His voice rose a little, growing friendlier. He leaned in closer, lowering his voice again. He smelled kind of nice, like saltwater and rain and fresh air. "I had my skimnet in the perfect spot, just a few spans downstream from the first outflow on the outgoing tide. The reservoir was filling up fast—it always surprises me how inefficient their process is, to be honest. Anyway, I thought it was a mouthfish at first, until the tentacles unfurled."

He described it feeding in much the same way as in the book, stunning the fish somehow and sucking them in "like a bucket of smooth, purple flesh with a beaked mouth this big at the center, filled with tiny teeth." He formed a circle with his thumbs and middle fingers. "The smaller one, presumably the male, examined my net, then flashed colors at the bigger one before disappearing into her skirt."

He shook his head, eyes wide with disbelief. "The way she looked at me..." He held out his hand as if grasping at smoke. "There was an intelligence behind those eyes, more so than most people, I'd wager." He clenched his hand into a fist, then let it drop to the table. "I think she dazzled me."

Seara let out a laugh that echoed in the empty room. She covered her mouth, then shared a conspiratorial smile with Cliff. "Me too. Only it was more like...she calmed me." That feeling she'd had under the dazzler's gaze was more peaceful and restful than any night's sleep she'd ever had. Certainly more restful than the dwindling amount of sleep awaiting her at home. Hopefully Da's reservoir wouldn't run out; it had taken her an entire day to clean the place up after the last time. "Listen, I gotta go soon, but there's something else." She pulled the book toward her and flipped toward the back until she found the page about the sea snakes. Cliff leaned forward, brow furrowed as he studied the illustrations.

"Did you see one of these too?"

"No. Yes. I'm not sure." She tapped the paragraph about the giant congrid and slid the book toward Cliff. "I saw something in the outflow the other day, must have been fifty spans at least, with a mouth like this." Cliff looked up from his reading, eyes widening as she stretched her arms as far as they would go, from her shins to above her head. "Big enough to eat a dazzler."

"Or a person." Cliff's eyes fell to the table. "So, you're saying that a giant snake or congrid fifty spans long lives in the Trench?"

"I doubt it lives there. Comes hunting, more likely."

"Must have run out of food wherever it lives if it's hunting in the city." He tapped the table with his fingers.

"My thoughts exactly. Same for the dazzler. Which means—"

"We destroyed their habitat."

Seara shook her head. "Not we. *They*." She tapped the patch on her uniform. Stormchain.

Cliff sat back, face growing slack as he stared at the high ceiling with its recessed dwemer lights shining down. "The dazzlers came for the dwemer."

"And the congrid came for the dazzlers."

Cliff sucked his teeth. "Not only for the dazzlers."

"How do you mean?"

"A skimmer disappeared from the Trench a couple of weeks ago. Left no trace except for a puddle of blood. Splatter even hit the roof of the tunnel. I *knew* it couldn't have been the dazzler. She doesn't have the teeth to do that kind of damage." He flipped back to the dazzler's page and stared at it.

"Listen, I've got to go, but the book has another twelve days before it has to be returned. You can borrow it if you want."

Cliff shook his head. "I'll just study it here for a while and return it for you. It wouldn't be safe where I live."

Seara didn't ask, but it was probably one of the encampments along the Trench in the lower city, the ones that flooded every few months. The paper said over twenty thousand people lived there, which was hard to believe, but with times as tough as they were…

"That's fine with me. I trust you."

"Trust me enough to meet up for tea some time?" Cliff asked, almost apologetically.

Seara considered for a moment. It hadn't sounded like a romantic invitation, but with men, you never knew. Or rather, you almost always did, and it was seldom anything good. But their conversation had left her tingling with excitement—not for romance, but for what the two of them knew, the secret they held together.

"Tea sounds good." She ran through her schedule in her mind. "How about on Riverday at the teahouse on campus, the Fishwife? I work the night shift at the plant, so I can meet you after. Say, four bells fifty?"

"Riverday, four bells fifty. I'll be there."

As she stood, her mind spun with the dozen tasks she needed to complete before her midnight shift. Cliff stood with her, awkwardly holding out his fist. She bumped it with hers, then turned and left, feeling invigorated in a way she hadn't since before Da got sick. She hardly noticed her sore feet or her gnawing hunger as she made her way back home just after tenth bell. Once she'd fed Da and cleaned up, she should be able to get a solid chunk of sleep before her midnight shift.

Felice, the building manager, greeted her at her door with a mop, bucket, and red-faced scowl. "Your Da left the water on again."

Seara's heart sunk like an anchor. "Oh, gods, I'm so sorry, I—"

"Water leaked through to the bathroom ceiling downstairs. I'll send you the bill." She dropped the bucket and mop at Seara's feet with a clang. "And I'll be forced to send you an eviction notice if this happens again."

Seara nodded, closing her eyes to try to hold in the tears, to no avail. She sniffed noisily, then opened her eyes and picked up the bucket. The floor of the entry-way was wet and streaked, and she saw her only towels on the floor outside the bathroom, soaked with filthy water.

"Look, I know it's hard looking after your Da." Felice's voice was softer now. "Might want to try to get him a spot in the Works House. I got a friend who—" She stopped as her eyes met Seara's again. She shook her head, sighing through her nose. "Just think about it, okay?"

Seara nodded, then stepped over the threshold into the wet, stinking mess of her apartment. "Thanks," she called over her shoulder.

"Mind your step," Da called from the couch, looking up from his orb for a moment. "Someone left the window open. Rain got all over." He turned back to the globe, which was green now, headed to yellow. "Yellow," he said, tapping the globe with his fingers. "Gonna be orange soon."

"And then red," Seara said, squeezing dirty water from the mop and taking a first swab at the entryway.

"'Member that red hat your mother used to wear?" He glanced over, face lit up with amusement. "I always thought she looked cute in that. Oh! Orange! Getting close now." His face slackened as he turned back to the globe.

Seara's tears mixed with the gritty gray water on the floor as she mopped and squeezed, mopped and squeezed, squeezed, mopped and squeezed.

SEVEN

S ef's belly ached with hunger, but she sent as much dwemer as she could muster to her pads. Kin fed gently, carefully, occasionally releasing to suck in a stray wisp that slipped out. Gone were his greedy slurps, his tentacles wrapped around her pad like he was trying to squeeze her dry, the waves of unbridled joy he'd send her as he fed. Their bond had been so strong back home, only a few moon cycles away from communion. She'd been sure of it. The humans had taken that away in a day when they'd capped the vent with that huge metal dome and that infernal pipe stretching all the way to the surface.

She and the other cuttlers had tried to pull it apart, but it was tougher than a ravager's back. They'd been making a little progress on one of the seams, she thought, until the humans had sent down divers with dwemer-powered spears and nets. They killed three cuttlers, and before the reef community had a chance to mount a counterattack, the ravagers arrived, feasting on human and cuttler alike. If only the ravagers had the wit to realize what they'd done to their own home...

Sef pushed more dwemer to her pad, though Kin was hardly drinking. He was so considerate of her reserves that he was going to starve to death. *"Drink,"* she said, turning her pad pink. Kin released her duct and floated to face her, still holding on to her pad with one little tentacle. He was purple with concern.

"Don't hurt yourself to feed me. I'll be fine."

She flashed red all over for a moment, then toned it down to her sunset pattern, adding a little extra pink, since Kin seemed to like that. *"We'll go get some more silversides today by the power plant. They fill me up pretty well."*

"Not well enough." Kin's colors shifted to match hers.

"Enough to get us by for now."

Kin pulsed red for a moment, then shifted slowly toward blue, his pensive color. The blue lightened the way it did when he got an idea, turning almost white for a moment. *"I'll drink if you let me go back and look around the power plant a little more. I need to figure out why they have all those screens in place. Why they're so worried about a few little fish getting in there."*

Sef felt herself rushing to red, but she tempered it with tiny dots of yellow to orange it out. *"Kinnikins, it's too dangerous. If anything were to happen to you and I couldn't—"*

Kin released, pulsing to float right between her eyes. His body practically glowed red, and his tentacles were as dark as the deepest abyss. *"STOP. TREAT-ING. ME. LIKE. A. SQUIGGLER! I CAN TAKE CARE OF MYSELF!"* He pulsed backward, staring at her angrily for a moment before mirroring her red and yellow pattern, a sign that he didn't want to fight. She sighed out a pulse through her siphon. He was right. He might be small, but he could defend himself, and he was as slippery as an eel when he didn't want to be caught.

She swapped the yellow and the red, then let herself return to her sunset pattern again. He stayed in his pattern a little longer, then mirrored hers again as he pulsed back to her pad and wrapped one tentacle around it. His eyes stayed with hers as he latched on again. He flashed brilliant blue with lavender spots as he began to suck, harder now, hard enough to stir a tingle in her gut. He gripped her pad with his tentacles, plastering his body to it as he sucked so hard it hurt in the best possible way. She closed her pad around him, tightening their bond further, letting his feelings flow over her. His concern for her. His respect for her. How beautiful she was to him.

How much he wanted to *be* her.

She pulled her pad into her mouth, aching from Kin's now ravenous feeding. His need flooded her mind as she closed her mouth around her pad and slowly increased the pressure. His pleasure rose the tighter she gripped him, so tight she was worried he'd pop—which is exactly what he did, releasing his ink into her mouth as a wave of euphoria roiled through her mind, flushing the despair from her hearts and sending tingles down to the tip of each tentacle.

She slowly released the pressure, pulling her pad out and opening it right in front of her eyes. Kin swayed in the faint current of their corner of the wreck, eyes half-closed, his body the gentlest lavender with light pink bubbles all over.

"I love you," he said.

"I love you more."

"No such thing. That's reef madness you're talking."

"That's because you drive me to distraction, love."

Kin flashed white with amusement. *"We'll call it a draw."*

"A truce. I aim to prove it to you once and for all once we've found our place. Together."

"Together."

Sef watched nervously as Kin slipped through the gate and disappeared into the dark tunnel. He'd shared a mental image of what he'd seen beyond the channel, but it was unnatural and confusing, even for a human construction. She *might* be able to squeeze between the bars, or possibly bend them, but it was far from a sure thing. Any damage she caused could alert the humans to their presence, which was the last thing she wanted.

Except maybe the dwemer collector, assuming that's what they were doing with that strange device. They'd seemed all right. Curious, even, once they got past their initial panic. And the person in the boat had seemed to *see* her in a way she hadn't expected. Sef had only seen humans from a distance until a few moon cycles ago, but their ruthless plundering of the oceans made it clear what they thought of her kind. Neither of the two humans she'd allowed to see her seemed like the sort who would cap a dwemer vent or trawl the ocean floor with huge, weighted nets, scooping up everything in their path. They were the same species but with very different values, much like cuttlers from far-flung reefs.

Focus, she reminded herself. She positioned herself so she could see both the canal and the outflow channel equally. She assumed the form of the muddy bottom, straightening a couple of her tentacles into rigid mossy sticks like the ones that littered the canal.

She released a thin, steady stream of scent dampener, hoping it would mask her presence in case another ravager was on the prowl. She could hold her own for long enough to escape, assuming she had sufficient dwemer for a stun pulse. She wasn't sure she could outrun a ravager, but she should be able to get far enough away to find a hiding spot and wait for it to rush past.

But she wasn't going anywhere without Kin.

EIGHT

Kin munched on a lone silverside he'd found by the grille closest to the power plant. The humans' movements were fairly predictable. A small group of them moved back and forth between the towers and a door, occasionally talking or working together on something. Two more patrolled the perimeter of the pool in opposite directions, shining their lights into the water, presumably looking for stray fish. They each carried a net on a pole, which one of them used to pick up a bit of debris from the water and toss it aside.

He'd worked out that the water came into the pool from an opening to his left, just out of sight. It was channeled toward the blue-tinted glass and steel towers, then released, warmer than the water in the Trench, and with a tantalizing hint of dwemer. Of home.

The lights on the ceiling, the ones carried by the guards, the boats that moved faster than wind—all of it was powered by dwemer. Kin couldn't understand how they did it, but humans were clever builders, able to compensate for their weak, inflexible bodies by shaping the world for their convenience. However their dwemer machines worked, they had destroyed Kin's home to power them. Human machines, it was said, were powerful but delicate constructs that could be disabled by finding and destroying the right part.

He waited until the guards were at their farthest from his position, then peeled back the corner of the screen. He squeezed through the opening and plastered himself to the wall just outside the grate, assuming its exact color and texture. Sef wouldn't have been able to hide this well; sometimes being small was a big advantage.

Once the guards passed again, he sank to the bottom of the pool and swam along the wall in the direction of the channel where the water was coming in. He stuck close to the wall, using it to slow himself when the current increased near the inflow. He merged with the bottom as the guards approached, though between the turbulence here and his camouflage, there was little chance they'd see him. The water coming in was from the river, but it had been filtered somehow. It had no more dwemer than the trace amounts found everywhere. It flowed into a channel that seemed to lead directly to the tanks. He took a moment to summon his courage, then pulsed out into the current.

It was stronger than expected, but he quickly found the opposite wall and hopped along with the current's help, stopping every so often to make sure he didn't lose control. The channel divided in two, one part veering to the left and the other continuing along the wall. One for each tank, he presumed. He launched himself at the corner and gripped the wall where the two channels divided.

The current battered him, but he'd faced worse during storms. He couldn't see well in either direction, but what he did see seemed to confirm his hypothesis. One tower loomed above him, directly over where the channel veered off and became a tunnel. The other was visible in the distance as a hazy blue shape, in the direct path of the other channel. However they were processing the dwemer, they needed clear water to do it.

He inched his way along the tunnel's wall, his eyes adjusting to the darkness. He could *feel* the dwemer from here, almost overwhelming in its intensity. The current picked up as the tunnel narrowed into a large pipe, made of metal, which thrummed with deep vibrations from above. He held fast to the smooth surface with his suction cups, sending out a ping to get a feel for what was ahead.

The pipe turned upward and appeared to split into four smaller tubes that fed into the tower. They were more than big enough for him to fit into, but he worried the water might be flowing too fast for his cups to hold him in place. He flattened himself as much as he could and advanced one tentacle at a time, using more and more of his cups as he approached the divide.

The water battered his skin as it flowed by. He crept closer and closer, feeling the strain on his cups, but as long as he kept flat, he could hold on. The pipe was immaculately smooth, which helped; the humans must clean it periodically to prevent algae from growing on it. The unnatural thrum from above grew deafening, like one of the humans' giant dwemer-powered boats. He crept closer to the divide, his whole body vibrating with the current and the machine's thrum. As he neared the closest tube opening, he positioned all his tentacles behind himself for maximum hold against the current. He just needed to get his head around the edge of the tube and send out another sounding pulse to see what was inside the tower.

As his head poked over the edge of the entrance, the pressure suddenly increased, and his suction cups slid along the smooth metal. His head ached from the battering of the water; he tried to pull back, but one of his cups released, then another. One tentacle released, then a second, and in an instant, he was sent tumbling up through the tube.

He had no chance of holding on to anything as his body shot up the tube, battered by the current and the walls. He managed to curl himself into a ball as the tube seemed to spiral ever upward, like the coils of certain corals. He slammed into a metal wall, the pressure of the water behind him forcing his body through a much smaller hole, which looped around and around. Everything hurt as his body was pressed through the tube, which seemed to get tighter and tighter. Just when he was sure he was going to be crushed to death, he popped out into a wider tube rushing up up up. He remained in ball form, eyes shut as he banged against a wall and was shot into another spiral, this one wider and faster as he descended.

The thrumming was all around him, as was the dwemer's blazing aura, which he would have recognized anywhere. There was no doubt this was from his home vent. He had no time for nostalgia as he spun faster and faster, growing dizzy and faint. He uncurled for a moment to take in water as he hit a small chamber where the current slowed.

He held himself in place with his tentacles and saw a thick glass barrier leading to a chamber with a tube of glowing blue liquid running down the center. Hundreds of wires ran along the tube, all leading to a black square with big red symbols on it. The current tugged on his tentacles; he could hold here but was eager to be free of the noise and vibration of this metal tomb.

He curled back up and was sucked into a wide tube and flung down below.

He ricocheted through the tube and shot out into the water, barely alert enough to match his color to the gray of the fabricated stone. He unfurled, seeing the glowing blue and shiny silver of the towers behind him as the current pushed him toward the outflow. He caught himself on the wall and molded himself to its texture, giving his hearts and gills a chance to bring him back from the brink.

If the humans had noticed his exit, they showed no signs of it. The guards continued their predictable circles around the pool while the others clustered around the base of the towers as before.

"KIN!"

Sef's thoughts hit him with the force of a crashing wave. She wouldn't risk such a shout for nothing. He hurried to the edge of the grate and squeezed through the corner of the screen he'd peeled back, then shot downstream, pulsing with all his might. He saw a shape out of the corner of his eye that might have been a human above, but he didn't slow down to find out. He squeezed past the second screen, not bothering to replace the corner he'd pried free, and through the other grille to the edge of the canal. He positioned himself just on the corner and sent a quick sounding pulse downstream.

"I'm here," he whispered. Sef materialized right in front of him, mud-colored like the bottom of the canal. She scooped him up in her pad and tucked him into the folds of her skirt, then turned and pulsed away. Soon they were flying down the canal and into the bay. Sef's mind was as impenetrable as a sea turtle's shell, but he could feel her fear and anger in her jerky motions. She finally slowed once they reached the flats, then stopped after some repositioning.

"Kin, I was so worried." Her thoughts were shaky, erratic, like she got when her dwemer was low. *"I thought I'd lost you."* She slowly unfurled her skirt, releasing Kin into a pocket in the seathorn, as protected as they could get outside their reef.

He shot up in front of her, turning his softest green. *"I'm okay, Jelly Belly."* He flashed pink for a moment, then back to green; no sense risking a color display with ravagers on the prowl. She cupped him gently with her pad and brought him right up to her eye.

"You're hurt."

"Not really." Now that she mentioned it, he did have some sore spots, but nothing was cut or ruptured. *"I got bounced around a little, is all."*

"Bounced around by what?!?" Her panic was rising, bringing out red dots all over her body.

"I went inside the dwemer machine! I spiraled up and up and down and down, and there was this horrible thrumming, worse than the biggest dwemer-powered boat. And then I got spit out at the bottom and floated back on the current."

"You went inside the dwemer machine?!? Kin, you could have been killed!"

Kin flashed red for a moment, then back to a darker shade of green. *"I told you I can take care of myself! I'm not an egg that needs to be constantly tended!"*

Sef's shade softened, the red dots fading, her skin taking on the same tone of green as Kin. *"You're right."* She turned blue, then violet for a moment. *"I'm sorry."*

Kin pulsed forward and plastered himself across her face, his skirt covering one of her eyes. *"I accept your apology. Now, can I tell you about my plan?"*

"Your what?"

"I saw something. Inside the tank." Red spots bloomed amid the green on Sef's body. She wasn't going to like it, but he needed her with him on this. He stood astride her eye, as he did when he was extra serious. *"I think I've figured out a way to break their machines."*

NINE

Cliff arrived at the Fishwife early, but he circled the block a few times instead of sitting down. He hadn't been to a proper teahouse in years, and the dishwashers probably wore nicer clothes than he did. When he saw Seara approach, his heart lurched; he'd half expected her to stand him up.

He wouldn't have blamed her. He looked like he lived in a tent in the lower city and washed his clothes in the Trench. She was wearing a different uniform this time, well-worn forest-green pants and shirt with a matching waxed seacoat. She looked tired but determined, a steely gleam in her eye that inspired a fierce little burst of pride in his chest.

"Cliff! Sorry I'm late. I had to get a new reservoir for my Da." She bumped fists with him and angled her head toward the entrance.

"I've got nothing but time." That wasn't strictly true; the low tide was approaching, so he'd miss the best time for skimming, but he wasn't in much of a hole at the moment. Assuming the tea wasn't too expensive.

A hostess swept them through the crowded interior and led them to a cramped table in the corner, which appeared to be the only one left. If she judged Cliff for his clothes, she showed no sign of it. "Your server will be with you shortly." She smiled and was off.

Cliff squeezed into a rickety chair with a thin pad on the seat, back against the wall without much room to maneuver. He studied the place as Seara took off her coat and hung it on the back of her chair. Several dozen tables were crammed into the space, with an open window to a kitchen filled with steam and occasional bursts of fire. It looked to have been an old warehouse or machine shop, with painted metal poles holding up a thicket of beams near the high roof. A spiral staircase led to a balcony with dozens more tables. The smell of tea, pastries, and something savory filled the air, accompanied by the roar of countless conversations and the clatter of the kitchen.

"It's great, right?" Seara was beaming. She'd hardly cracked a smile at their last encounter.

"It's amazing," Cliff said, despite feeling buried in an avalanche of sensations.

"We used to come here all the time. Me and my Da, that is." Her smile faltered for a moment. "We should get our order ready. They serve fast here."

"What do you, uh…" Cliff looked at the enormous chalkboard sign above the window to the kitchen, which listed more than a dozen teas, as well as spirits and a dizzying array of food choices.

"Good afternoon, fellow humans." The server was short and fat, with light blue streaks in their hair and multiple piercings across their cheery face. "What can I get for you two today?" Cliff glanced at the board in a panic. The words swarmed around each other like silversides, shifting and indecipherable.

"I'll have the redbird, sweet and frothy. Same for you?" Seara eyed Cliff encouragingly.

"Yes, one frothy redbird for me as well." He'd never heard of redbird, but frothy sounded good.

"And a small breadboard, unless you're really hungry?" Seara turned to Cliff, who shook his head.

"That'll be plenty, I'm sure." In truth, he *was* hungry, but not for food you had to pay teahouse prices for.

"All right, I'll bring you out two redbirds and a breadboard. We have smoked quinn and honey butter today."

"That sounds lovely," Cliff said to their back as they bustled away. "That sounds...lovely," he repeated to Seara, whose indulgent smile took the steam out of his utterance. "That's fish, right?"

"Cheese," she said with a kind blink. "Hard, but somehow creamy at the same time."

"Oh," Cliff said, unable to imagine what that would be like but salivating at the chance to find out.

"The board's on me," she said casually, though she clearly wasn't that much better off than Cliff.

Cliff's cheeks flushed, but he smiled and nodded. "I appreciate it. I'll get it next time." He flushed further, his hands fumbling to make a gesture of contrition. "I mean, if...that is, if we ever—"

"Sounds good." Something about her voice set him at ease. She clearly led a stressful life, but she showed such kindness, such empathy, such...kinship, almost. She knew what it meant to lose what you had, how close everyone was to the edge.

"So, you used to come here with your da, huh?" Cliff felt a little awkward asking, but she'd mentioned him.

"Every Starday. He always drank blackbird, no cream, no sugar. 'Like a sailor,' he'd say." Her smile was wistful with a sliver of joy. "When Ma died, we didn't come as often. And then he got the torp."

"I'm sorry." Cliff had seen it in the camp, people who just stopped going to work, stopped talking, stopped eating unless someone made them. There were clinics uptown with medicine that slowed it, but there was no cure. Eventually people just forgot to breathe. "How long..."

"Two years, more or less. He still has his good moments, but..." She trailed off as the server arrived with a large cutting board spread with several kinds of bread, a generous amount of cheese with an or‐ange-brown rind, and two tubs of what might have been honey butter.

"Two redbirds, extra froth, and a board. Anything else?"

Cliff eyed Seara, who smiled and shook her head. The server disappeared with a wink. The smell of sweet spiced tea hit his nose, and Cliff stared down at the mug, filled to the brim with foam, with sprinkles of something brownish on top. Seara picked up her mug and held it out to clink. Her eyes closed as she took the first sip. All the tension seemed to drain from her face as she put it back down. She licked the foamy mustache from her lips and opened her eyes.

"Exactly like I remember."

Cliff took a careful sip, which was tricky due to the thick layer of foam. The tea was strong, sweet, and creamy, with hints of spices: nutberry, windseed, and something earthy he couldn't quite place. He wiped the foam from his mustache with a napkin.

"Mmm, this quinn is to die for." She'd already but‐tered a piece of bread, laid a slice of cheese on it, and taken a big bite. Cliff did the same. It was surreal, eating in a restaurant, even if it was just a teahouse. Having someone serve him, treat him like a person instead of just an annoyance. And the way Seara talked to him, how at ease she was; he hadn't felt that way since—

"So." She took another bite, wiped her hands on her napkin, and pulled out a notebook. "About our tentacled friends." She'd made a list, and what looked like a map. "I saw one out in the flats, about here." She tapped a spot on the map with her finger. "And you saw one in the Trench, about here, right?"

Cliff tapped his finger next to hers. "Yes, exactly. Right by the first outflow from the power plant."

"Which is the same place I saw the giant congrid. I've done a little more research and I'm sure that's what it was, not a snake."

Cliff took another sip, staring at the map. "So, the dazzlers hide out in the seathorn there, but they come up in the Trench to feed on silversides and such." He traced the path with his finger.

"That's my theory. And the congrid's probably hunting them, along with mouthfish and whatever else is in there."

"Mouthfish," Cliff murmured. Something tickled his brain. He saw them all the time when he was skimming, sometimes as long as he was tall. They never bothered his net; they just swam up- and downstream, occasionally thrashing at the surface. Flipping off parasites, one mouthfisherman had told him. He hadn't seen that guy in a while. Hadn't seen many mouthfish lately, either. "Come to think of it, they aren't as thick in there as they used to be."

"A congrid that size could whittle the population down in no time. Haven't seen many on the flats either."

"I wonder why the congrid came to the outflow. You said it attacked the gate?"

"I figured it was after me. You said something killed a skimmer a while back, right?"

"Louie." Cliff had never liked Louie; he tended to hog the good spots and stay there smoking after his reservoir was full. But he was funny sometimes, and he'd helped Cliff out with a part one time when his skimmer broke. Something sparked in his mind, and he snapped his fingers. "It's the dwemer."

"The dwemer?"

"In the water. The power plant releases enough for me to fill a reservoir in half a bell at low tide. And I saw the dazzler eating silversides, which are always there as well. Come to think of it, I don't recall seeing that many before the plant was there."

Seara wrote the word 'silversides' in her notebook and circled it. "Now that you mention it, they're normally an ocean fish, as far as I know. A lot of fish can move back and forth, so it's not too surprising, but..." She tapped the pencil against the notebook for a while. It was hypnotic, one regular sound amid the chaos of the teahouse. She stopped suddenly, speared a hunk of cheese, and popped it into her mouth. She closed her eyes, face soft with pleasure. When she opened them again, they practically threw sparks. Cliff raised his eyebrows, and she took a sip of her tea before continuing.

"I just remembered, they're *reef* fish. Just like the dazzlers. And I bet you..." She picked up the pencil and circled the words 'dazzler' and 'congrid,' then drew lines between them to form a rough triangle. "I bet you a hundred marks the giant congrid are too."

"The dwemer vent," Cliff said quietly, picking up a slice of bread and buttering it carefully.

"That's where the dwemer in the plant comes from. I bet the silversides feed on it, or feed on whatever tiny creatures feed on it. The dazzlers eat the silversides, which must accumulate dwemer in their bodies. It would explain the dwemer wave communication and the other supposed powers the dazzlers have. And the congrid eat the dazzlers."

"They all need it to survive, and—"

"And we destroyed their habitat. Now they're desperate."

Cliff's heart sank at the thought of dazzlers fleeing their dying reef, dodging congrid and daggerfish and gods knew what else. Whatever dwemer they could get from the silversides at the outflow couldn't be enough to sustain them for long. "That's terrible" was all he could muster.

"It is."

They sat in silence for a while, or what passed for silence in a room echoing with dozens of conversations. They polished off the board and their tea, and the server returned with fresh mugs before they even thought to ask.

"It doesn't cost extra," Seara assured him.

"Oh, no, I didn't..." He stopped at her kind smile. She knew what he was thinking, that five marks for a mug of tea was an incredible extravagance, one he couldn't afford to repeat. He took a half-hearted sip, then perked up as the sweet, spiced tea flowed into him. He smiled at Seara, only to see her eyes sparkling once again. "What?" he asked. He loved her energy. Whatever she said, he was on board.

She shook her head, still smiling. "You're going to think I'm crazy."

"We wouldn't be here if we both weren't a little bit crazy."

She took a long sip of her tea, then set it down and tented her fingers. "You want to go on a boat ride?"

TEN

Cliff was waiting at the dock with his ratty skimmer bag, looking around guiltily and making himself small. Seara had seen the look plenty of times, people acting like they were worth less just because they had less money. She felt the same way every time she went to the university, a mop among brooms. Not all students were rich, but most of them were uptowners. They were nice enough, making polite small talk before class, but it always felt like they were doing her a favor, or storing up goodie points for their dinner parties.

"There's this real nice downtown lady in my life sciences seminar, always wearing one uniform or another. I guess she's working two jobs and still finding time for

her studies. So admirable." She had a sudden urge to spit. When Cliff raised his hand and smiled at her, she had an equally sudden urge to hug him.

"Thank you for lending us your expertise, Cliff. This is Ray, who swabs the deck while I steer."

"I'm her boss." Ray switched his bag to his other shoulder and shook Cliff's hand. "I hear you're the dwemer expert."

"I wouldn't go that far." Cliff looked equal parts embarrassed and dubious. She couldn't believe he'd agreed to go along with this harebrained scheme.

"Well, if Seara vouches for you, that's more than good enough for me. Shall we?" He gestured down the dock, and Seara fell in behind him with Cliff at her side. Cliff seemed to study the boats as they passed, paying special attention to the big dwemer-powered rescue boats with their shiny steel and hardened glass reservoirs.

Seara took the front, and Cliff sat quietly in the back while Ray readied the oars. Ray untied the boat from the cleats and pushed off with little ado. Moments later, he had powered them out of the little harbor and into the lower Trench.

The tide was going out. It would be low in a bell or so, stay that way for a little while, then come rushing back in much faster than it had gone out. They'd be out for at least 3 bells; in a boat like this, they had to come and go with the tide, as there was no rowing against it. The air grew saltier as they approached the bay. Ray maneuvered them between larger boats and the occasional floating log, and soon they had escaped the main channel.

"The seathorn flats are over there," Seara called over the squeak and groan of the oars. "We'll go straight to the place where we saw it before and work our way along the edges."

Cliff nodded, eyeing Ray, who seemed lost in the rhythm of rowing. Cliff probably wondered how much Ray knew; she hadn't had time to explain it all to Cliff. The subterfuge of the dwemer measurements was for the benefit of anyone who might wonder why the conservancy was bringing someone like Cliff on their boat. Ray had been skittish after their encounter with the dazzler, but he'd agreed to go along with it.

"All right, slow down and pull the oars," Seara said quietly as they entered the flats. They could pole their way through from here, which should make them stealthier, not to mention better able to see through the surface of the water. It was always fairly clear around the seathorn, which might explain why the dazzlers liked it here.

"Might as well go ahead and check the dwemer levels while you're out here," she said to Cliff as she assembled the pole. "I've been curious, to be honest." She anchored them in the seathorn, and Ray pulled the paddles and stretched side to side.

"My gauge is busted, but I can do it by feel." Cliff pulled a tangle of poles and wires out of his bag and put them together with practiced ease. She'd never seen a skimnet up close; it wasn't that different from a fishing net, besides being made of copper and steel. The handle looked to have been made from scrap fencing or maybe a signpost, with a standard reservoir inset below a battered dial. "All right, I'll just dip it in here..." Cliff lowered the net, watching the water and angling the pole. "Okay, let's see." He closed his eyes as if in concentration. A glass chip inset next to the dial glowed weakly. Ray watched with obvious interest, possibly tempered by skepticism.

Cliff opened his eyes, twisting his mouth sideways. "It's about a decile over neutral, less than half what it is in the Trench. I guess the effects of the power plant are diluted here." He started to pull the net out, then stopped, staring off into the distance for a long moment.

"What?" Seara asked, her curiosity piqued by Cliff's slightly raised eyebrows.

He turned toward her, mouth quirking into a half-grin. "This reservoir is half full. I could release the dwemer the same way I extract it."

"And maybe attract any dazzlers in the area. Yes, do it!" She glanced to Ray for approval.

He smiled nervously. "Are we sure they won't want to..." He sucked in through his teeth, shaking his head a little.

"They won't," Seara and Cliff said at the same time. Cliff blinked at her to speak.

"They'll be curious, maybe even grateful. It's dwemer they need, more than food. They can catch fish easily enough on their own. Remember last time? How all it did was look at us for a bit?"

"You mean when it gave me an attack of the wheeze?" His face paled a little, and he slipped a hand into his pocket.

"You have your breather?" He nodded. "And you know what to expect this time. Just keep it handy."

He didn't look convinced, but he nodded, pulling it out of his pocket. "Okay, but you owe me." His voice rose to a point as he spoke. "I'm talking a full shift where you cover for me."

"Whatever you need, Ray." She hated the idea of lying for anyone, but none of that mattered. She *had* to see it again.

Ray sighed through his nose. "Okay."

Cliff looked to her for approval. She nodded, taking in a big breath and letting it out slow. "Do it."

Cliff lowered the net back into the water, closing his eyes again. Was the device somehow more than mechanical? There were tales of storm shamans and mystics who could control dwemer with their minds, but it had always seemed like fairy tale stuff, or science masquerading as magic. Cliff turned the dial, and a smile slowly grew on his face.

"I've never actually done this before." He opened his eyes, but they were distant, as if his mind were elsewhere. "It's going out. Which way's the current flowing?" Seara gestured past the front of the boat. "I'd keep an eye out in that direction," Cliff said.

It didn't take long for the water to come alive. Silver flashed in the water ahead as small fish began swirling in an increasingly long area down current. The water rippled and splashed as larger fish knifed in, feeding on the agitated baitfish. A huge, dark shape rose from the seathorn, showing a fat side of yellow gold; a scupper half the length of their boat began feasting amid the chaos. The trail of activity showed like a stream amid the flats as the dwemered area spread and divided.

"I'm going to slow it down now," Cliff said, ducking his head to study the reservoir and adjusting the dial slowly. "I want to make this last, and I think we've made our presence known."

"We have at that." Ray's voice was oddly serious. He stood, picking up the harpoon and pointing to the water ahead.

"Ray, what are you doing! We're not trying to kill it! We're—" Seara's voice trailed off as she saw it: a long, sinuous shape more than fifty spans in length, undulating toward them at remarkable speed. Flashes of silver and panicked splashes spread before it as the congrid picked up steam, its mouth opening to show rows of long, clear-gray teeth.

"Rotate us sideways!" Ray shouted. Seara grabbed the pole and pushed off in a panic, losing the seathorn and sending the front of the boat into the current. Ray was shouting, "Get down! Get down!" but Seara was frozen, unable to move or take her eyes off the toothy monstrosity churning its way toward them. Warmth ran down her leg and a tear down her cheek as she saw her death coming, body crushed between the creature's deadly jaws, flinging red froth—

A great flash lit up the water, blinding her and sending her tumbling backward. A thud echoed in her head, and darkness swallowed her.

ELEVEN

Kin shot out of Sef's skirt as she spread her body wide directly in front of the charging ravager and flashed white all over. Kin had flicked his pupils shut enough to avoid being blinded, but the ravager roiled to a halt, gnashing its teeth and whipping its tail around. Sef grabbed hold of the tail as it hit her, and she disappeared as the beast whipped it back. Kin seized the moment, pulsing right in front of one of its eyes and blasting it with his strongest sting. He barely made it out of the way as the ravager's head thrashed, its vicious teeth cutting nothing but water in its blind fury.

He hovered just out of reach, awaiting another opening. The creature's body undulated in an unusual way, muscles rippling from back to front. Kin prepared to fight or flee, hearts racing as he realized it was Sef, pulling herself up the length of its body by her tentacles, her color matching the eel's green-gray hue as she moved. The ravager's massive body coiled around, tail slapping at her, trying to dislodge her. When its head stayed in place for a moment, Kin pulsed in again and zapped the other eye. This time, the creature's entire body spasmed, shaking Sef loose and sending Kin hurtling backwards. Another wave pushed him farther away as the creature thrashed once more, then disappeared into the now churned and muddy water.

"My love," Sef said, cupping him in one of her pads and tucking him into her skirt.

"I'm okay," he assured her with a mind-pulse. *"And you?"*

"I'm fine. And it's gone, for now."

"I gave it something to remember me by. Zap! one eye, then Zap! the other!"

Her mind-voice was silent for a moment. Instead of the expected admonishment, she said, *"My little warrior."* Her mind warmed, but worry remained. *"It will return. We need to get gone."*

"What about the humans?"

"They'll have to fend for themselves."

"We need to tell them!"

"Tell them what, Kin?"

"About their dwemer machines! About our reef!"

Her mind went dark for a long moment. They were moving, slowly, though she wasn't showing him where. She stopped, worry leaking through her silence. *"They probably won't be able to understand us."*

"Not with that attitude!" He pressed against her skirt, which she opened enough to let him out. They were not far from the boat, whose oars had just splashed back into the water. He swam in front of her, flashing orange on the part of him the humans couldn't see. *"Let me try!"*

Sef freckled with red dots which quickly disappeared. *"I'll be right with you. If they so much as look at you wrong—"*

"I know!" He didn't need her to take care of him; hadn't he just fought off a ravager mostly on his own?

Her concern melted into him. She wanted to protect him. He understood the feeling all too well.

When he thought of how she struggled to produce enough dwemer for him, how she deprived herself to feed him, he was ready to take on an army of ravagers. Anything, everything, to find a safe place with plenty of dwemer for their communion. He flashed pink on his face for her, then turned and swam over to one of the oars, which hung just underwater. He took in a long jet of water, then gripped the oar and pulled his head just above the surface.

There were three humans on the boat: the one he'd seen with the dwemer net in the Trench and the two he'd seen on the boat before. They all stared at him, none of them moving. He opened with a mind-wave of welcome, which he matched with his green hue as he sent out the peaceful greeting. The humans immediately relaxed. Good! This was working!

Kin slowed the welcome and pushed out a link wave, hoping at least one of them would be able to connect. There were legends of humans who could communicate with cuttlers; storm shamans, they were called. They sailed out in boats with metal spires atop them and channeled dwemer from lightning, somehow containing it and saving it for later use. They would speak with the cuttlers as they waited for the right conditions. Many a night as a young squiggler, Kin had listened to the tales of the storm shamans, the many wonders and terrors of the human world above.

He felt a weak connection with one, the dwemer collector, and another, the one in the boat who'd stared at them with such curiosity out in the flats. The other merely gazed, mouth half open, and held the oar still. Kin slowly climbed up the oar, waving two of his arms in peaceful curves in front of him. There was no way to know if they understood his gesture, but the connection with the dwemer collector deepened.

They emitted a series of sounds that must have been language. Kin responded, *"I do not speak human language."*

The man—Kin was sure somehow that this was a male of the species—touched his head, glancing at the others, then approached, crouching for balance in the awkward craft. "You do." The man emitted sounds that must have been speech, but his meaning reached Kin's mind as it would from a young cuttler just learning to speak, or one from a faraway reef.

"Good. We understand each other. I must be quick, before the ravager returns. The dwemer in the big tanks in your city was taken from—"

"Your reef!"

"You knew?" Either humans were smarter than they were given credit for, or he was involved in the theft of the dwemer.

"We figured it out. I've never heard of dazzlers—that's our word for your species—entering the city before. You kept coming back to the power plant outflow for the same reason I did: for the dwemer. And that's where they get it from. The reefs." Kin hardly noticed the man had stopped vocalizing and was speaking mind to mind with remarkable aptitude. Good. Maybe they could work together after all.

"They took our home." Kin flashed red, and the man holding the oar jerked back a little, causing the oar to sway. Kin returned to a serious blue. *"They're going to pay."*

The man rubbed his face for a moment, then explained what Kin had said to the others. A conversation ensued, and when the woman looked at Kin, their connection suddenly clicked.

Her first thoughts were garbled; she was moving her mouth but only gibberish came through their mind link. She closed her eyes for a moment and stopped vocalizing. When she opened them again, they blazed into Kin's, and her speech came through clearly. *"Tell us how we can help."*

TWELVE

Seara watched Cliff walk away, leaning a little against the weight of his bag, but with a lightness in his step. They would meet for tea again tomorrow and plot their next moves. The idea of helping the dazzlers take down the power plant and uncap the dwemer vent had her head spinning with possibilities. But first, she had to go home and make Da dinner and then hopefully get a couple bells of sleep before her night shift. No rest for the angels, she supposed.

Da was asleep on the couch, the Fascinator cupped in his palms. He looked so old, his wrinkles standing out all the more starkly in the globe's changing colors. His face twitched each time the color changed, and when it came to red, he smiled, though his eyes remained closed.

Seara chopped an onion as quietly as she could and tossed it in a heating pan along with a drizzle of oil. She added a bit of diced hard sausage, then a can of brown sauce, and set it to simmer while the stale bread crisped in the toaster.

"Seara? Is that you?"

"I'm here, Da. Just making some crust and sauce."

"Smells good. Orange!"

She put the back of her knife hand to her forehead, taking a long, slow breath in and out of her nose. "Gonna be red soon!" she called.

They ate in silence on the couch, staring at the globe. After she'd finished feeding him his crust and sauce and eaten her own, none too hot by the time she got to it, she noticed Da glancing over at her during the blue and green phases.

"Something on your mind, Da?"

He raised his eyebrows, still staring at the globe. "You seem different."

"Different how?"

He turned to her during the next blue phase, a gentle smile growing on his face. "You seem happy."

Seara leaned in and hugged him tight, holding on extra long to hide her tears. She released as the orange lit up the wall behind him. They watched it turn red together like they used to watch the sun rise across the bay on their early morning fishing trips. When it returned to purple, his body slumped, and he sat silent for a long moment.

"Don't much care for purple," he murmured, grunting when it phased to blue. "Can't be red all the time, I guess."

Seara studied the towers during her rounds. She'd never been all that curious before; they'd always just seemed like giant machines to her. Which they were, of course, but how did they *work*? A pair of sturdy pipes led in from the wall, splitting off to each tower; presumably one was for unprocessed dwemer, the other to move the finished product into the storage tanks somewhere beyond the door. Above the pipes was a big glass window where technicians sat staring at something. Dials and levers, she imagined, probably some blinking lights, like the controls at the base of the towers.

Guards weren't allowed past the yellow painted lines on the floor, ten spans or so away from each tower, continuing to the wall on either side of the metal door where the technicians came and went. The machines gave off a constant hum, which she usually tuned out after a while. It was a deep, smooth vibration, like something heavy spinning at high velocity. On occasion, it would slow down and start rattling, and the technicians would adjust their instruments until it returned to its normal pitch.

She got the stink-eye from the lead technician, so she returned her focus to the pool. Guards weren't supposed to get too curious about anything except the water. There was nothing in it, of course, not even a minlet. Most days, there wasn't, but apparently if something the size of a silverside got through, it could cause all kinds of damage. She volunteered to check the screens, which gave her some alone time. That was how she liked it, and why she liked working with Ray. He knew when to shut up.

The screens were intact. She could still see the fold where the outer screen had been peeled back and returned to position. A rat might be able to peel it back, but not return it so neatly into place. Other than a human, she could think of only one creature able to do that. *Kin*.

The name swam in her mind, an image like a curl of seaweed, compressed into a shape and sound she could understand. It fit him somehow; he was small, but his intelligence was no less sharp for it. Sharper than hers, most likely. And brave, too; he'd gotten right up in the giant congrid's face and flashed it several times until it finally fled. The powers these creatures had were so far beyond what humans were capable of, it was hard to fathom. What other mysteries lurked in the undiscovered depths?

Legends told of creatures in the deep sea older than human civilization itself. Some believed that all life, including humans, came from the excretions of such a creature, slumbering atop a dwemer vent, its massive body covered with forests of coral and brilliant anemones. Others said the world itself was its dream, each soul born anew every night only to be extinguished at sunrise. She liked that version best. In that version, the Da she knew wasn't slipping away forever. He was drifting patiently toward rebirth.

A splash in the Trench sent her heart racing. A mouthfish trying to knock off parasites, most likely. Probably not a fifty-span congrid looking to bust down the gate and make a meal of her. She returned to the pool room and continued her rounds. Kin would be able to make it through easily enough, especially with the distraction of the silversides once he pulled a wide hole in the screen. She wasn't sure exactly how he planned to take down the tanks; something to do with the inductors Cliff was supposed to acquire. *Just help me get in safely and I'll do the rest*, Kin had said.

She hoped he knew what he was doing. She was putting a lot on the line for him, or rather, for them; the much larger female had lurked nearby during the whole interaction but hadn't communicated with them. How were they even the same species? She was a hundred times bigger than him, if not more. How did dazzler sex even work?

The idea of intertwining tentacles got her a little more bothered than it should have, especially at work. It had been far too long since she'd had anything except for her fingers. And even if she met someone, could she really have sex, knowing her father was staring at his Fascinator in the next room?

She'd entertained the thought of getting together with Cliff. He was a sweetheart, he wasn't bad looking, and he was clean, for someone living in a tent in the lower city. Most importantly, he wasn't a creep. She wondered, though; if she dropped a few hints, would he even notice? Even on her worst days, men would look at her a certain way, but he never seemed to. Even men who weren't attracted to you checked you out. Maybe he was gay, but...she didn't get that vibe either. She sighed as the manager gestured toward the intake tunnel with their eyes. It was always wet and slippery in there, and half the lights were broken.

She walked with careful steps, keeping a hand near the damp railing. The concrete wasn't that slippery in and of itself; patches of moss hidden by the shadows between the lights were the real danger. She'd slipped and nearly broken her tailbone a year ago and been off her feet for several weeks, none of it paid. She couldn't afford to go through that again, and there was no one to take care of Da if she got hurt.

She bet Cliff would help if she asked him. He was the closest thing she had to a friend at this point. Except maybe Ray, but as close as they were on the boat, they'd never once seen each other outside of work.

She dragged herself home, stopping to pick up a couple of sausage rolls for breakfast. She hated eating like this, but she had to take care of Da and then wash up before she went out to meet Cliff. Not that he would care, but she always felt dirty when leaving the plant, even if she hadn't done anything messy.

Da was in a good mood, asking her questions during the purple and blue phases and holding his teacup on his own. When she told him she had to get washed up and go out, he cocked his head at her and cracked a tiny smile.

"You gonna meet up with that fella again?"

"Yes, Da, but it's not like that."

"If you say so." He raised a finger as yellow faded to orange. "Here it comes," he whispered, touching her knee just as he used to after seeing a faint tap on the line when fishing.

Seara laid a hand over her Da's and watched through tears as the orange blurred to red.

THIRTEEN

Cliff watched Seara weave through the crowd as he stood under the little awning of the Fish-wife. Her face lit up in a smile when she saw him. She gave a little wave, which he returned with a smile of his own. His heart warmed to see her; at this point, she was the closest thing to a friend he had. To his surprise, she took his shoulders and kissed the air around his face, brushing against his freshly trimmed beard. She smelled like soap and drizzle, with a whiff of something musky and flowery. Was she wearing perfume?

"Great to see you, Cliff!"

"You too, Seara," he answered, pulling the door open. "Looks pretty crowded."

"It always is, and they always find you a seat." She raised her eyebrows and held up two fingers to the hostess, who nodded and signaled to someone across the restaurant.

"Right this way." She gestured with one arm toward a server, who hustled toward them.

"Welcome to the Fishwife! If you'll follow me?"

They sat, and Seara ordered the same thing as last time, two redbirds and a board. "Unless you want something different?" Cliff shook his head. "And some water, if you don't mind. Thanks!"

She turned to Cliff, folding her hands together on the table. "So..." Her eyes were bright with anticipation. She looked around, leaning in a little as she continued. "This feels so weird, but nobody can hear us above this din." She gestured around at the scores of customers.

"*I* can barely hear us above this din." It felt so strange, sitting across from a woman in a teahouse, having a conversation. Like he was living a different life, the one he might have had, but for a few wrong turns and strokes of bad luck.

"Right? Okay, so let's go over the plan." She pulled out her notebook and flipped to a page with a roughly drawn map on it. "Stop me if I get anything wrong; the whole thing was kind of confusing." He was glad she'd said it; the experience of talking to the little dazzler mind to mind was a bit of a blur. "Phase one. This is the power plant, or at least, the part of it relevant for the plan." The map showed the Trench on one side, with the first outflow channel leading up into the plant itself. He'd always wondered what they did in there, what it was like. "Kin will enter here, pull back the screen, and do something to attract the silversides. I don't know what exactly…"

Cliff nodded. "He's going to dazzle them and use them for cover."

"Of course! Did you get the inductors?"

"I did, and cheap, too. Traded for a length of insulated wire I had stashed away." He fished them out of his pocket, nervous about showing them in public, not that anyone would care even if they knew what they were. He hoped the magnets would be strong enough for the job.

Their hands brushed as he dropped them in hers. It was always strange, touching another person. He went days, even weeks without doing it. Mostly, he didn't mind the lack, but with Seara, it was nice. Nice that she didn't see him as untouchable, as many up-streamers would. And nice because he liked her. He hoped she didn't expect anything more, but that was a bridge to be crossed another day.

She hefted them, seeming satisfied. "He should be able to carry these, right?"

"I sure hope so, because those are the smallest I could find." They weighed about two pebbles apiece, which shouldn't pose much of a problem, even for a dazzler as small as Kin. She handed them back, and he pocketed them, sweat breaking out in his rain-dampened clothes. Why was he so nervous?

"Okay, so, you drop the inductors to Kin, who'll catch them. Then he goes off and does his thing." She lowered her voice and leaned in close as she said it, as if they were conspirators in some great perilous venture. Which, in fairness, they were; if Sef and Kin succeeded, they'd cause untold millions in damage to Stormchain's infrastructure and choke off the city's supply of dwemer for quite some time. Cliff had done his best to tell Kin what to look for, though in truth it was mostly guesswork. No one knew how Stormchain processed the dwemer, but it would take current to do it, and a strong enough magnet would scramble the converters. In theory.

Seara snapped her finger in front of Cliff's face. "Got something to say?"

"No, just...I hope I told Kin enough. I don't really know how those things work, and I was just guessing. I hate the thought of—"

Seara's second snap stopped him cold. She wore a stern but friendly smile. "I prefer to focus on what we need to do and leave the rest to the Elder Being." Her hand fell on Cliff's, warm, reassuring. "Did you do the best that you could in a very strange and fucked-up situation that came upon you without warning?"

Cliff's frown crept toward a smile. "I guess I did."

She leaned in close again. "Did you talk to a damned dazzler with your *mind* and explain to it how to disable the converter?"

He couldn't suppress a full smile this time. "You know what, I did. I did that."

"How many people could have done what you did?"

Cliff put up his hands in surrender. "Okay, you win. So I drop the magnets to Kin—"

"And you hustle down to the dock to meet me."

"You got the dwemer boat?"

Seara bit her lip as if to keep from smiling. "Told them we're after dazzler hunters. Rumors have been going around about people seeing them in the flats. That's a ten-thousand-mark fine, and a big prize for the conservancy. Let's hope they don't fire us when we come back empty-handed with a half-drained reservoir." She quickly flipped the notebook closed as the server hurried up with their drinks.

"Board will be out shortly."

"What's the side today?"

"It's your lucky day. Fresh mouthfish roe." Cliff's mouth watered. He hadn't had roe in years.

"Perfect. Can't wait!" Seara blinked at the server, who disappeared with a quick smile. She turned back to Cliff, eyes wide with excitement. "Where were we?"

"I was about to express my concern over the risks you're taking. I don't have a job I can lose, not as such, but you..."

She waved him away. "The security job will be fine. They'll still need security even if the plant breaks down. No way they could pin that on me, or anyone for that matter. And the conservancy, well..." She threw her hands in the air. "I'm not going to lie, I love that job, but it doesn't pay much. Half the time we're just spinning our wheels. The problems are so much bigger than us. This is a chance to do something real, something that *matters*. What are we conserving, if not the homes of creatures like the dazzlers?" Her voice rose as she finished, her eyes shining bright as stars.

"If you're sure." Cliff smiled at the server as they brought the tea.

"I'm sure." She took the mug in both hands and took a sip. "Mmm, this really does take me back."

"How's your Da?"

Seara set down the mug carefully and licked the froth from her lips. When she looked up at him, her eyes were hard but warm, her expression full of the good-humored attitude toward suffering that seemed to be the city's specialty. "He's got his moments." She turned the mug in a circle on the table. "He asked after you."

Cliff touched his chest. "How'd he know to do that?"

"I told him about you. A little bit, anyway. Sometimes it seems like he's not listening. Other times he only seems to hear what he wants. He called you 'that fella.' He seems to think we're dating or something." She dipped her spoon in the froth and lifted it to her mouth, glancing up at him in a way he didn't know how to interpret. "Anyway, some days he doesn't say a word except to name the colors on his Fascinator, so any talk is good talk."

Cliff took a careful sip of his tea. This was why he didn't spend a lot of time around people; he was never sure what he was expected to say. "That's good, I guess." Some people used Fascinators to keep their children quiet while they did chores and such; it made sense that they'd work with the torp as well. "Those things are hard on the dwemer, I hear."

"Why you think I got two jobs?" She chuckled through her nose. "Anyway, it's just me and him, ever since Ma died. It's better than sending him to the Works House."

Cliff hummed his assent into his tea. He'd slept there on occasion during cold snaps. They did their best, but it was a grim existence, and none too safe. "He's lucky he has you."

"And I'm lucky to have him, though it doesn't always feel that way." Cliff pretended not to notice her pulling out her handkerchief to dab her eyes. "Anyway, I sketched a copy of the reef map from the library." She opened her notebook back up and flipped through until she found a page with a map showing the bay, with Umian on one edge of the map and the open sea on the other. Several areas were marked with little illustrations of coral, anemones, fish, and even what looked like dazzlers.

"I like your drawings."

She sniffed a laugh. "I got that from my Ma. She could draw anything, sing anything, played half a dozen instruments, too. I only got the drawing part. Comes in handy once in a while in school."

"You studying to become a doctor?"

She let out a *psshh*. "I'm not that smart, or that rich. I'm in the nursing program, but we have to take the same first year as doctors. Or first three years, in my case, since I'm going part time. Only five more years left."

Cliff was glad for the arrival of the board, as the thought of planning his life five years ahead sent him into a tailspin. He was lucky if he could think five days ahead. "That's some commitment."

"I'd be done already if it weren't for..." She shook her head as she grabbed a slice of toast and spread a dollop of creamy white roe sauce on it. "Mmm, you've got to try this." She held one hand cupped over her mouth as she spoke while chewing. "Anyway, like my Da always said, 'Nobody can live your life but you.'" She dusted her fingers, still chewing, and plucked what looked like a pickled baby onion off the board.

"I guess that's the truth." A truth that made Cliff a little queasy, looking at the way he lived his life. But what choice did he have, in a city that paid its workers so little while charging impossible amounts for the bare necessities? He shook his head to clear it and studied the map.

A rectangle sat in the middle of a large reef at the end of the bay. A wiggly line ran from the middle of the rectangle down to a circle in the reef with little dots like rivets around the edges. Seara's drawings of coral looked flatter there, and there were hardly any fish or anemones. "So that's where the dwemer vent is?"

"Mmhmm." She tapped the rectangle. "I've never been out that far, and they keep boats at a distance, but I hear it has a large floating platform for boats to dock to. I imagine we'll know it when we see it." She lifted her finger and set it down on a little boat drawn next to a tiny dock at the edge of the city, which she'd represented as a group of crowded rectangles with the Trench dividing it. "The dwemer boat's on the north dock. My calculations make it about a ten-league trip each way. The reservoir's good for fifty, so we should have no problem getting there and back. We're going to chase down any hunting boats we see out on the flats, partly for show, and partly because fuck anyone who hunts osmo or dazzlers."

Cliff was surprised at the burst of vulgarity, but it made him like her all the more. "No argument from me on that."

"We'll check registrations and live-wells, give them something to tell their buddies, maybe keep a few of them away for a while. Once the flats are clear, we'll shoot out past Sharprock Island here." She pointed to an island drawn with a little tree growing out of a boulder. "From there it's a straight shot down the middle of the bay. I figure the platform will have lights on it, so we'll be going dark for the last league or so."

Cliff bit his lip. This could be dangerous. Stormchain wouldn't leave such an important installation unguarded. "I expect they have patrol boats keeping watch."

"For sure, not to mention a navy frigate, from what I hear. We're not going to get too close. Kin and Sef will swim in from there and...do their thing." She held her hands wide, then pressed them against the table. "I get that Sef's going to try to destroy the pipe somehow, but I didn't quite catch what Kin was going to do to the platform. Did you?"

Cliff nodded. It had been a blur of images, but he was pretty sure he'd understood the gist. "I didn't catch all of it either, but he asked how they store the dwemer on the platform." He lowered his voice and leaned in. "I told him I assumed it was hardened glass tanks, and he got real excited. I gather he thinks he can break the glass somehow, causing a chain reaction, which in theory..." He made an explosion gesture with both hands. "Whatever they're doing, I'm guessing it'll be obvious if it works." He picked up a piece of toast and spread some roe on it, leaving the last portion for Seara. "I imagine once we drop them off, we can head back any time."

She spread the last of the roe on the last piece of toast. "I, for one, want to see what kind of damage they can cause." She bit into the toast aggressively, then slowed as her eyes closed and a beatific expression spread over her face. "I haven't had roe like this in *years.*"

Cliff nodded as he chewed, savoring the burst of salty, creamy goodness and the toast's perfect crunch. He washed it down with the last sip of sweet, milky tea. It was going to be hard to go back to day-old sausage rolls and Mae Kambal's musty tea after this. Seara was staring at the map, hands balled into fists on the table. Something about her had hardened after their encounter with the dazzlers.

"Not to pry, but…" Cliff nodded as the server replaced their empty mugs with freshly frothed and steaming ones, then whisked away the board before he knew what had happened. "When it…talked, what was it like for you? Did you hear…words, or…"

Seara sipped her tea, staring out the rain-spattered window. "It took me a moment, but I got most of what he said. Or showed; some of it was like pictures. I got lost a few times."

"Yes! It was weird; part of it felt like words, but some of it was…I don't know how to describe it. Images, underwater sounds, *feelings*, like he was sharing his thoughts and emotions directly? It was…it was a lot."

"You're like a storm shaman," she mused, lifting a spoon of foam into her mouth.

"I'm like, an eighth of a storm shaman, tops."

Seara snorted a little laugh. "I don't know, I'd give you at least a quarter. Between the dwemer stuff and talking to dazzlers? All you need is a tattered cloak and a boat with an antenna." Little did she know that it had always been his dream, but the gears of progress grind ever forward, leaving the ruins of the past in their wake.

"Maybe I was born in the wrong century." Cliff's mind spun as he sat with that thought for a moment. What would Umian have been like a hundred years ago? The air might have been worse, since dwemer power would have been in its infancy and blacktar powered the city back then. The first storm towers were built during that time; there was even still a functional one near the tip of the peninsula, maintained now more as a museum than as a power source. The storm shamans would have been fighting the inevitable tide and losing. Cliff thought of the few lessons he'd been able to afford, back when the price of dwemer was skyrocketing and some thought the shamans might make a comeback.

"Osmo got your tongue?"

Cliff shook his head, unsure if it was worth telling her. When he looked up into her eyes, that doubt fell away. She wanted to know what he was thinking.

When was the last time he could say that about someone?

"I took some lessons from a storm shaman when I dropped out of school, must be almost twenty years ago now. I had a few marks left over from my stipend, and I thought it sounded cool. You remember the dwemer shortage?"

Seara laughed through her nose. "We were cooking with blacktar inside the house for a while. Fucking grim."

"Right?" It was around that time that he'd moved to the lower city, to a tenement without dwemer or water. It was cheap, but after a time, it had made more sense to sleep for free in a tent. "Anyway, there was this guy in the lower city who'd go out on his rickety little sailboat into a storm and come back with three or four tanks of dwemer. I chatted him up, and he agreed to take me on as 'an apprentice,' for a fee, of course. It was cheaper than university and it looked like he was making out all right."

"You sailed with a real-life storm shaman?"

"Sailed, yes, a couple of times. We never caught a storm, and I ran out of money quick. But the skills he taught me helped me learn how to skim, which is better than nothing." Not much, but still.

"And helped you talk to dazzler! Besides, any job is a good job in this infernal city. The Stormchain execs living uptown burn through more dwemer than the rest of the city combined, and we're down here fighting for scraps." Her voice took on an angry tone as she continued. "They pillage the reef and destroy creatures more wondrous than they could possibly imagine, all for a few toys that make their lives a little bit easier." She was practically growling now; Cliff thought the people at the next table might have been listening in, but Seara clearly didn't care. "At this point, I don't give a fuck if I lose my job. I'd rather live in the Works House than help these vultures get richer by making people like my Da sick."

Tears streamed down her cheeks. She held her cup in a white-knuckled grip. Cliff slid a hand across the table, not daring to touch hers, but he left it lying nearby just in case. One of her hands slipped off the mug and clamped over his, and the other moved to her face. She sobbed silently, gripping Cliff's hand tightly.

Tears rose in his eyes as well; he turned his hand over and held hers gently.

He hoped this was the right thing to do; he felt like it was what someone would do in a book. She squeezed back; her hands were warm and damp, more calloused than he'd expected. It made sense, given the type of work she did.

She withdrew her hand slowly, blinking a smile through tears as she pulled out a rumpled handkerchief and made noisy use of it. "Sorry, I don't know why I got so upset all of a sudden."

"You've every reason to be upset."

"I guess we both do." She sniffed and wiped her nose again. "But whatever we feel, it can't be half of what Kin and his ladyfriend are going through."

Chills crept up through Cliff's body, turning to fire in his heart. "And that's why we're going to help them get their life back."

FOURTEEN

*C*ome on! Kin flashed in a low-light spectrum that humans wouldn't be able to see. *"The coast is clear!"* He beckoned from the edge of the boat with a tentacle, then skittered out of the way as Sef hauled herself up onto the wood and metal craft.

It took her eyes a moment to adjust to the world above. Things always looked oddly wavy at first when seen through the air. Kin was right; the dock was empty, though the lights were brighter than she'd have liked. It was hard to fathom using dwemer to power lights at an unoccupied dock, especially in a city where some people were pulling trace dwemer out of the water to stay alive. Maybe that was why the pair had agreed to help them. She kept still, matching the color and texture of the boat automatically. Kin had climbed up on the boat's cabin to watch out for intruders. He flashed her a burst of green to let her know it was safe, then went dark again.

Sef positioned herself atop the glass and metal tank, which was about the size of her core. She could feel the dwemer within, but she could not smell it. She wasn't sure how they kept it in, or what would happen when she opened it, but she was desperate. She could hardly swim, and her signals to Kin were getting weaker and weaker. It took her a few moments to figure out how to unfasten it; it was a complicated mechanism that took more strength than expected.

It opened with a *whoosh*, and a blast of cold buffeted Sef's belly until she got her mouth open and clamped down around the opening. In an instant, she was sucked away in a dark undertow, tumbled across the ocean's deep, ballooned by almost orgasmic tides that stretched her like a jellyfish. She floated above her reef now, as it was before the humans ruined it, body surging with life as the vent flowed freely into the dark water. Schools of fish darted to and fro en masse; eels poked their heads out of the crevices of vibrant corals; anemones, sponges, and fans glowed in all their bioluminescent glory. Her mind filled with color and sound and light that were so intense it was almost painful. She gave in to it, let it wash over and through her like the breath of the Elder Being itself.

A faint tingling sensation drew her from her reverie. It repeated, more of a sting now. Was something biting her? She lashed out with a tentacle to dislodge whatever it was, and a distant voice pierced the cacophony of her senses.

Who was calling to her? What did they want? Her hearts raced with panic as she realized what the voice was, *who* the voice was.

"Sef!"

It was Kin. He was in trouble. *"I'm coming, baby."* She gathered her tentacles beneath her, but they were so clumsy, twisted together like a mass of sea worms.

"Sef! Let go! You have to let go!" Kin's voice echoed in her mind, but it made no sense. Let go of what? She was floating above the reef, but it was dark now, gray and black, with the bleached skeletons of coral gleaming sickly out of the darkness. A deep thrumming sounded, coming from a huge metal dome right

in the center of the reef, with a thick pipe twisting its way toward the surface. What was this thing, and what was it doing in her reef? Another jolt pierced her mind, sharper this time, like the sting of a lightning fish.

"SEF! LET GO OF THE NOZZLE! YOU'RE GOING TO—"

The world came rushing back in, along with a burst of cold dwemer steam. Sef slumped to the deck, tentacles twitching uncontrollably. Her mind struggled to process what had happened, what was happening; the steam slowed, then stopped with a *clunk*. Kin was on her face in an instant, perched high on his tentacles so both eyes could peer into hers. He looked ominous from this position, judgmental. He flashed yellow, then orange, then red, cycling through the pattern several times before relaxing to blue.

"Are you okay?"

"I'm fine, I just..." The dwemer lights along the dock twinkled and spun into fractal patterns that were so beautiful she almost forgot where she was. *"The dwemer..."* The dark flush in her hearts spread across her body, turning her black as midnight. It took some

effort to shift to a dusky violet for Kin's sake. The taste of home filled her mouth, even as its absence grew inside her like a sinkhole.

"It was from our reef." Kin darkened to match her. *"I could tell. Even just in the time it took me to wrestle the cap back on, which, yes, I did all by myself, thank you very much."* He fluttered to pink and back as he finished, to make it clear he was joking.

"You're so strong." The tip of one of her tentacles wrapped around him. He turned scarlet as he fought to escape her grip, then yellow for an instant as he shocked her and slipped from her grasp. *"Ow! And you fight dirty."*

"I fight to win." He flared brilliant blue, with red around his eyes and at the tips of his tentacles. *"Now let's get out of here before somebody sees us."*

Sef sent another sounding pulse into the water around the abandoned dock, which provided adequate shelter; not what she would have preferred, but it was better than swimming out to their shipwreck and back. She doubted its thicket of half-rotted beams would stop a ravager, but she hadn't sensed anything bigger than a speckletail nearby. The ravager should have no reason to bother with this shallow inlet.

Kin was nestled in her skirt, sending clouds of joy into her mind each time he wriggled against her folds. When she opened up, he flitted right up to her left eye and began pulsing from blue to red. Perhaps it was the excess dwemer flowing through her system, but his colors seemed especially vivid tonight. He attached to the side of her head, still looking her in the eye as the speed of his pulsing increased. One of his tentacles snaked toward her siphon, which flared at its approach.

Kin had this way of undulating his tentacles; the prick of his suction cups releasing and reattaching in rapid succession made her want to open her siphon like a mouth and suck him right in. Sef quivered with delight as his tentacle slipped inside it, then another on the opposite side, stretching her wide. He looked her in the eye, then disappeared from sight as he lowered himself to cover her opening.

Kin's eagerness filled her mind as his tentacles encircled her siphon, pulling her rim taut in a way that was almost painful. She'd always imagined this was how it would begin. Their communion. They'd pleasured each other many times, but they both knew anything more than a tentacle into the siphon was off limits for now.

She'd heard stories of the intensity of the experience, the loss of self as two bodies merged fully, permanently. Kin opened his beak and ran his rough tongue along her rim, sparking a cascade of little tremors, magnified by his suction cup pattern. All it would take is one good pulse of her siphon and she'd pull him right in. She wanted that, wanted *him* in a way that sent electric shocks down to the tips of her tentacles, but now was not the time.

Someday. When they were safe.

Sef brought her own tentacles into play, planting a suction cup gently atop Kin's head as the tip of another caressed his sensitive skirt. She couldn't see his colors because of the angle, but an undersea garden bloomed in her mind, every color of the reef and some in which no creature had ever dared to drape itself. She nearly sucked Kin in when the soft head of his hecto probed the thrumming walls of her siphon, dangerously close to the sphincter leading to her core. She tightened from within, closing herself off as his head poked against her over and over.

"Hold on, sweetie." She narrowed her siphon around him. A shuddering built up from deep within as Kin sent little shocks against her sphincter, nearly forcing it open. Her mind flooded with his pleasure and she squeezed him until he popped out, leaving a trail of spent seed and ink in his wake.

Sef's pad caught him on instinct. He snuggled in as she half closed it around his soft, now-warm body. She felt the dwemer leaking out of her even before he fed. His beak retracted, and his feeding tube latched onto a duct with such hunger it stirred her again. She closed the pad tighter; he clamped down harder, sucking like a lamprey, beak pinching her hard enough to draw blood. Her mind exploded with sudden ecstasy, and her body followed, surrounding them both in a cloud of ink so black she could no longer see the city's lights.

Her pad released, and Kin glommed onto her face in the darkness, tentacles draped around each eye and along her forehead.

"I'm scared, Sef," Kin said after a while.

"Me too." Scared for what Kin was about to do. Once he went past the grate, she couldn't protect him. And out on the reef, even if they were successful, there would be casualties. The ravagers could tear her in half and swallow her, but if she died knowing Kin had survived, it would be worth it.

"You don't have to protect me."

"I know."

"I like it when you do, though. When things get too big for me to handle, I like knowing you'll be there for me."

"Like you were for me when the ravager came for us."

"Always. I love you and I want to be part of you for-ever." Kin's thought reached her like a sudden stream of dwemer from an unseen vent. She basked in it, returning the message with the force of a storm swell.

"Until the oceans run dry, my love."

Neither of them spoke as Sef navigated the dark canal, alert for the telltale dwemer waves of a ravager. Her senses were so enhanced by having drained the tank that she could count the scales of each fish she passed. She moved upstream with little effort, helped by the incoming tide. Dawn was still a while away, but there was no room for error.

The human with the dwemer net stood just downstream from the power plant outflow, just as he'd said he would. Sef sent him a wave and watched as he perked up and fished something out of his clothing. She clung to the edge and extended one of her pads toward him. He approached hesitantly; as vulnerable as she felt leaving this delicate part of herself exposed, he must be doubly afraid of what she might do to him. She pushed out a wave of peace, which seemed to have its effect. His warm, ridged fingertips brushed against her pad as he carefully handed over the two metal objects. Their magnetism tickled almost to the point of pain, but she held on and sent a wave of thanks, accompanied by a brief message:

"See you at the island before dawn."

"We'll be there. Tell Kin good luck."

Sef sent a wave of warmth. She almost wished she hadn't let Kin do all the talking; there was a lot to learn about these humans. But not now. She sped to the outflow, scanning the area again before releasing Kin from her skirt.

He pulsed up in front of her and spread his tentacles wide. His color shifted from canal-brown to his battle mask, abyssal black with red rings around the eyes. *"I'll be back before you know it."*

"I'll be waiting." Sef tried to keep strength in her thoughts, though she felt as weak as a bagfish.

Kin took the magnets from her and blinked back to nearly invisible brown, shifting toward grey as he darted into the outflow. Sef let herself sink to the bottom. She didn't like being in contact with canal mud for this long, but there was nothing for it. She didn't *feel* any parasites digging into her, and there wasn't anything in this river that could truly threaten her except the ravager. She burrowed into the mud, using it for cover. Gods, she hoped Kin was all right. And she hoped he hurried up.

Fifteen

K in studied the guards as he clung to the wall just behind the screened grate leading into the pool. They followed the usual rotation, and after a while, he saw the one who could talk approach. Seara, she'd called herself. He flashed white for a moment, then faded back to the mossy green-gray of the wall. She stopped next to the grate and peered down into the water. He locked minds with her with minimal resistance. These humans were smarter than he'd given them credit for.

"Is everything in order?" he asked.

"All according to plan. Do you have what you need?" Her speech had improved dramatically.

Kin lifted the two tentacles holding the magnets, which were set in steel squares with holes in each of the corners, as if taken from a larger machine. One of them yanked toward the grate and locked on with a loud *clink*, though it wouldn't be audible to the humans above the sound of the dwemer machine. He had to brace four tentacles to pry the thing off, all while holding the other magnet far away from the grate. Seara sent out something like a laugh.

"It's fine. I got it." He cut off communication, which was a bit rude, but he had enough to deal with getting the magnets through the grate. Seara continued her walk. Kin peeled a corner of the screen aside carefully. The magnets were quite heavy for their size, and their dwemer signature was almost physically painful to touch. They kept sticking to the bars, so it took a bit of contortion and exertion, but he made his way to the other side of the grate before the next guard got close enough to see him. They'd be focused on fish, not a blob of moss on the wall. Once the guard had safely passed, Kin slipped below the current and let himself drift to the bottom, weighted by the magnets.

He inched his way toward the intake channel, moving awkwardly because of his irritating cargo. He had to stop several times due to the guards' rotation; when he saw Seara approaching, he took advantage and sped to the edge of the intake channel, then shot down to the divider and plastered himself against the wall in the dark tunnel leading to the first tank. The current was strong here, and he hated not having full use of his limbs. He stuck one of the magnets to a metal plate just inside the tunnel and lifted the other one to his beak. He couldn't afford to let it touch the steel walls inside the tank until he'd reached the vulnerable core.

Cliff had confirmed that the black box with the red symbols on it would likely be the weak point. All the wires led through it. According to Cliff, human dwemer use was constrained by the copper wires required to channel its power, which had to run through what he called a converter; if those were disrupted, the machine would stop working in a heartbeat. If he could brace himself against that opening and get a tentacle in, the magnet should disrupt the circuit and cause the whole thing to shut down. The way the tank was constructed, it would be difficult to fix, and he hoped it would cause some collateral damage in the process.

He approached the entrance, holding tight with all his tentacles to avoid getting sucked inside. He'd run through the layout in his mind a hundred times. He'd always had good spatial sense, and with as much dwemer as he had in him now, he could almost see the entire structure, recreated from memory. He had to hope it was accurate, and that he could stop in the right place, and that he could get the magnet in without getting zapped, and that the machine wouldn't explode while he was making his escape. And then he'd get to do it all over again.

This was fine.

He thought of poor Sef, half-buried in toxic sludge, waiting for the ravager to come and spoil all their plans. He liked to think that even if it showed up, she'd have an answer for it. They'd already chased it off once before; maybe it was afraid of them now.

Focus. Kin sucked in a few siphons of water, clamped down on the sharp edges of the magnet, and rolled into a ball as he entered the tube.

Though he had experienced it before, he still wasn't ready for the strength of the flow, like a giant rainbow shrimp's sonic punch. Starting in ball form helped, but the sharp edges of the magnet kept getting jostled against his flesh, cutting into his cheeks. He spiraled up until he hit the top, then began circling down, around and around at dizzying speeds, the thrum of the machine and the power of the dwemer vibrating through him like a leviathan's song.

Everything was too fast, and he kept spinning and spinning, bouncing and careening. His mind snapped to attention, and his tentacles followed, unfurling at just the right moment and suctioning onto the side at the intersection he remembered from before. He pulled himself out of the current into the little niche with the window he'd noticed last time, showing the brilliant blue dwemer tube with its myriad discs and wires.

He stuck the magnet to the bottom of the pipe and plastered his face against the window. This was going to be the hard part. The glass was thick, and no doubt strong. He couldn't get any grip with his beak to bite it, so he started tapping at it instead to get the resonance frequency. It was well within his range, especially as dwemered up as he was. He pried the magnet off the tube and held it aloft with some difficulty as he focused his mind on the glass. He closed his eyes and emitted a sonic burst.

No sooner had the glass shattered than Kin was forced through the jagged hole, shredding his skin as he floundered in the swirling waters of the quickly filling tube. This close, the dwemer was blinding, overpowering, like the euphoria of a violet ray's sting. He floated with the swirling water until the magnet clamped against the bottom of the tube.

The bubbles dancing in the blue blaze of the dwemer reminded Kin of the night migration of fire jellies. In the time before the humans had come, he and Sef would sit on their perch in the coral with their tentacles intertwined and watch them float by. His hearts swelled with this image of home.

Home.

With Sef.

Communion.

Kin squeezed his pupils shut and opened them again, clenching his beak as he strove to find purpose amid the chaos. He saw red, and something tripped inside him. *Red.* The symbols on the black box. It was just above him. He heaved the magnet off the floor and crawled slowly up the wall; the swirling water wouldn't have been difficult in normal circumstances, but he could barely feel his tentacles in his dwemer fugue. He flopped up, one suction cup at a time, until the tip of a tentacle touched it.

It was warm; that had to be a good sign. He maneuvered himself just above it, suddenly exhausted from his endeavor. He lifted the magnet and lowered it slowly toward the black box. He had no idea what would happen once it touched, but he'd have to swim up and out through the little jagged window in a hurry. In his condition, that wouldn't be easy.

Sef.

Waiting for him, ready to take on the world with him. Ready to become one with him. His vision came clear in an instant. He lowered the magnet until he could feel it pull, then pushed off with all his tentacles as he released it.

He pulsed up and around the blinding shaft of blue dwemer, keeping a tentacle on the wall at all times against the unpredictable current and his own diminished capacity in this crucible of power and sensation. A shock ran through the water, not enough to stun him, but enough to push him through the broken window without much care for his already bleeding skin. A metallic groan reverberated all around as he balled up and slid out of the niche into the downtube. The flow of the water slowed suddenly, and the machine juddered to a halt. Kin shot out the exit hole and bounced off the stone bottom a couple of times before he unfurled and anchored himself in place.

Voices rang out from the room above, shouts of panic, he thought. He hurried against the current to retrieve the other magnet and sped to the intake of the second tank. He curled himself into a ball as he was sucked through, repeating the process as before. Thankfully, this tank had the exact same structure as the first. He could see the tube ahead in his mind, giving him plenty of time to open his eyes and stop by the glass window on this tank, which looked exactly like the other.

He broke the glass with a sonic wave, as before, only he was careful not to get sucked inside. Once the chamber was flooded, he lifted the magnet through and stretched his tentacle to maneuver it around the dwemer tube. He had to wedge his body partway in to reach, but he didn't get cut. The magnet found the box all on its own. The shock was stronger this time, but Kin managed to extract himself safely and was soon tumbling against the bottom of the pool.

The vibrations of the second tank grinding to a halt reached him through the water like a distant earthquake. All the guards seemed to have clustered near the tanks, so Kin was able to move quickly, darting with the current along the bottom edge of the pool until he reached the grate. He slipped through the opening he'd made in the screen and hung on to watch for a while. Smoke was pouring out of the first tank, white to begin with, then black. Humans ran to and fro like silversides in a daggertooth swirl, dipping hoses into the water and spraying down the tank. A crystalline *crack* sounded, and the second tower began to smoke. Kin sped off through the channel, hearts on fire, nerves crackling with terror and excitement. He sent a burst into the canal, hoping the ravager wasn't anywhere nearby.

Sef answered immediately. *"I'm here!"* Her dark shape materialized from the murky water, shot through with lines of red worry. He zipped into her pad, which closed around him and tucked him into her skirt in an instant.

"I'm okay! I'm okay."

Sef was already powering down the Trench. *"You're hurt."*

"Just a little scraped up is all. I'll be fine."

"Let's juice you up just in case." Sef's pad slid back into her skirt, already leaking dwemer. Kin latched onto it and drank as he'd never drunk before. Sef didn't usually like to feed him on the move, but he had to narrow his throat to keep from getting overloaded.

"Enough," he managed. *"Thank you."* He caressed her pad with his tentacles, sucking in the stray wisps of dwemer that still trickled out of her. *"We did it."* Kin grew drowsy after all the excitement and the dwemer. He nestled into her pad, which closed gently around him.

"I heard breaking sounds. I was so worried, Kin."

"I told you I can take care of myself," he said sleepily.

"I never doubted you for an instant."

"I did."

Sef squeezed him tight, and Kin drifted off as the sounds outside shifted from the echoey confines of the canal to the calm waters of the flats. Ravagers came to him in his dreams, but not to eat him. One lowered its head so he could climb on top; he held on to its bony spine as it descended into the ocean's dark depths.

Sixteen

Seara handed the paperwork to the dockmaster, who grunted and checked her off his list.

"Low tide's at tenth bell." He was gone before she could thank him. She nodded to Cliff, who stooped to untie the moorings in a way that showed he'd spent plenty of time on a boat. Ray had bagged at the last moment; *"I just can't,"* he'd said. Seara didn't blame him. If she were found out, she'd be lucky if all she lost was her job.

She couldn't stop revisiting the moment when Kin had shown her his reef in colors so vibrant it made her heart want to burst. She could feel it in that portrait, what dwemer meant to him, to his kind. It wasn't just some disposable magic to give flight to their fancies.

It powered the entire ecosystem, the *civilization* of beings on the reef. Not just dazzlers and osmo; even the giant congrid in all their ferocity were a marvel. Among the myriad strange and colorful creatures that made the reef their home, there were no doubt wonders equal to the dazzlers that humans were unaware of. Whether or not the sea floor itself was an ancient, sentient being, as some believed, the devastation her civilization had caused in its pursuit of dwemer was as terrible as any war humans had waged in their history.

She'd thought the boat would be difficult to handle, but the dwemer pump moved them smoothly in whatever direction she pointed. As they left the no-wake zone and she pushed it to quarter-throttle, she could see why the rich fell in love with these machines. Before she knew it, they'd reached the flats, and the boat slowed to a silent crawl with a simple tug on the throttle.

"I have to admit, this is a nice boat." Cliff eyed the controls, and a pang of something almost territorial swept through her. She shrugged it off; had she fallen under the boat's spell so easily?

She laughed, putting a hand on his arm. "I'll let you pilot on the way back, in the open water at least."

The hint of a smile formed amid his neat beard. He pointed with his chin toward the rim of pale pink on the horizon. "We're right on schedule."

She navigated the channels of the flats with surprising ease. The dwemer engine rendered the current nearly irrelevant. Cliff stood on the prow, holding on to the rail, eyes scanning the smooth surface of the water. There would be some chop once they passed the labyrinth of islands, but here it was calm enough that the wake of a giant congrid should be easy to see. She pulled through the narrow channel leading toward Sharprock Island and reversed the engine, bringing the boat to a near stop, though they drifted slowly bayward with the current.

"There." Cliff pointed to a clump of seathorn, which began moving toward the boat. One of its branches snaked out of the water and unfurled, a long tentacle with a floppy pad on the end, colored and textured like seathorn. The pad opened, and Kin pushed up on all his little legs, flashing bright green for a moment before returning to an imitation of the seathorn. Seara's mind relaxed as whiffs of Kin's thoughts filtered in.

"Thank you for coming." Seara's chest warmed with his emotion, which she could feel through their connection. Was this what the dazzlers' life was like, sharing every thought, every emotion, from mind to mind? They were clearly a more advanced species than humans. They didn't deserve what had happened to them.

"We're with you all the way." She paused, feeling slightly dizzy with the connection. She could feel Cliff, too, though he seemed content to let her speak for them both. *"Just tell me where to go."*

The wind lashed Seara's face as the dwemer engine powered them forward at a smooth, steady pace. The boat was big enough to handle the waves easily; almost too easily. It wasn't hard to see how someone could get used to this kind of travel.

She tried not to stare at the dazzlers, who sat in the open live-well. Sef's tentacles draped onto the deck, taking on its coloring, even down to the grain of the wood. Kin sat atop Sef's head, periodically slipping back down into the water to wet himself and spray water onto Sef's tentacles. He changed color frequently, as if by mood. To judge from the mostly bright colors, he was more excited than scared. He was confident, too; more confident than Sef, who did not connect to Seara directly, but whose worry was palpable. Cliff sat squinting at the horizon, occasionally turning to watch Kin, who never seemed to sit still.

"There," Cliff said at last, pointing straight ahead. Seara saw it too now, a squarish speck in the distance. "Gotta be a couple leagues away yet."

Kin urged her on. *"Get us as close as you can. In open water like this, we're more vulnerable."*

Seara continued until Cliff waved her to stop. She killed the engine with the flip of a lever, and they drifted to a stop. The constant rush of the wind while they were moving was replaced by the slap of waves against the hull and the cry of a seagull. The sun was warm, even if the breeze off the water was cool. She dropped anchor while Cliff readied his fishing pole. He'd taken the assignment seriously; he'd even brought a tin of what looked like cut-up squid to use as bait. She hoped Sef and Kin didn't take it personally.

"We'll hang out underneath the boat until the sun goes down," Kin said. *"Ravagers don't usually hunt this close to the surface, so we should be safe, but if you see us climbing back aboard, get ready to fly."*

Seara sat in the captain's chair while Cliff fished. The combination of the sun and the breeze was a bit much for her, and the half-open cabin offered some protection from both. Cliff caught a half-dozen pricklebacks, which he tossed into the live-well. "Gotta pay the rent on this fishing rig," he said with a smile. He was genuinely enjoying himself.

A lump formed in Seara's throat as she watched him fish; he was about the age her Da had been when he used to take her out. She'd pulled many a prickleback out of the bay, though they'd never gone this far out in the rickety little sailboat Da would borrow from a friend at the university. If she had a boat like this, she could take him out, even in his condition. Maybe his fingers would remember their old strength if they held his fishing rod again.

"All right, I think we've established a plausible reason for our presence." Cliff slid onto the bench across from Seara and pulled his bag out from underneath. "How about a late lunch?"

She accepted the sausage roll with a smile. It wasn't the freshest, and it was a little smushed from the day's travels, but she was hungry and hadn't thought to bring anything.

"You know, this really is a hell of a boat," Cliff said through a mouthful of sandwich. "Hard to believe how easy it was to get out here."'

"If Sef and Kin are successful, there won't be too many of these running around. Not for a while, anyway." Stormchain would be back to cap the reef again, or they'd find another reef. Of course, anywhere dwemer came out of the ocean floor, there would be a whole ecosystem around it, which they would destroy just as they had Sef and Kin's reef. But no one cared, so long as it was a thousand spans deep. Out of sight, out of thought.

"Maybe the storm shamans will make a comeback." Cliff gestured with half a sausage roll toward the blue sky. "All the dwemer we could ever need, free for the taking, with the right knowledge and skill."

Seara smiled wistfully. They both knew those days were long over. Even if a hundred shamans raced out into the bay at each storm and came back with tanks full of dwemer, it wouldn't be a fraction of what the reef produced. There was simply no way to harness nature's power at the scale required for a growing industrialized civilization without causing irrevocable harm in the process. Still, it was a beautiful dream; Seara pictured this fleet of cloaked shamans heading out into the pummeling rain, grim-faced but alive, so alive.

They passed the afternoon chatting over not much at all, as if they'd agreed not to focus on the turmoil ahead. It was nice, being out here with Cliff, just sitting and watching the waves go by. Cliff would occasionally rebait his line and catch a few fish before sitting back down in the shelter of the open cabin. "Always assume someone's watching," he said, though the patrol boats from the rig hadn't come within a half-league of them. They saw a few fishing boats, and one dwemer sloop raced by in the distance, kicking up a fan of white spray in its wake.

"It boggles the mind," Cliff mused, hand on his chin. "Imagine having the kind of money where you could burn through dwemer like that just for fun."

"It's probably one of Stormchain's execs." The kind who lived in the Enclave above Uptown and took cable cars to work.

"I expect they're gonna be pretty pissed tomorrow, if this thing goes off as planned."

"Your lips to the gods' ears."

Seara's mind warmed suddenly with Kin's connection. Part of the side rail rose in the air, curving slowly toward her. "Amazing," she whispered, leaning in close to the tentacle, which had taken on the tubular shape of the rail and even its metallic shine. The pad opened, and Kin flashed bright green for a moment before fading to midnight blue. The interior of the pad reflected the blue just like the chrome railing would have.

"It's almost time."

Seara nodded, turning to Cliff, who blinked acknowledgment. *"We'll loop back once we drop you, as if we're returning to town, then approach as close as we dare in the dark."*

Kin took on a purplish glow for a moment, then faded back to blue. *"I'll wait for Sef to do her thing down below before I try to blow the rig. If it works, you'll know it. If you don't see us soon after..."* He paused, his color darkening to almost-black, with tiny points of blue scattered throughout. *"Go home. Take care of each other. Live."*

Seara covered her mouth at the sob that surged through her. Could this little creature really destroy an entire rig? And if he did, how would he survive the blast? And what exactly would Sef be doing down below to disrupt an operation of this magnitude?

"You too." She reached out a hand toward Kin, who raised a tentacle and wrapped it around her pinky. Seara's heart melted as the tentacle unwound itself and returned to Kin. He flashed a warm pink for a long second, then went jet black with thick red circles around his eyes. The pad closed, and the tentacle, now the color and texture of ink being poured out of a

bottle, slipped off the side of the boat and disappeared into the dark waters.

Seara felt Cliff hovering close. She turned and fell into his arms.

"They're gonna be just fine," Cliff said into her ear, holding her tight. "You'll see."

SEVENTEEN

S ef tucked Kin into her skirt and moved in slow, steady pulses toward the platform. The ravagers shouldn't pick up her vibrations at this speed, even if they were hunting this high up. Kin's bright determination warmed her from within like a miniature sun.

"My warrior," she said, squeezing him tight.

"My queen." Waves of warmth radiated from his body and mind. Sef tried to hide her fear as she sent them back to him. Could such a small creature really destroy the biggest human-made structure in the ocean? Sef dipped deeper as a patrol boat neared, bright yellow dwemer lights scanning the surface before them. Once it had passed, she sped toward the platform, keeping deep enough that their

lights wouldn't reach her. Up close, it was unbelievably massive, almost as wide as the reef itself, but with such rigid human angles. How could something so enormous even float, being made of metal?

Beneath the platform, lit up with their harsh lights, was the pipe leading down into the darkness. She hadn't had a chance to look at it since coming up with her plan, but what she saw confirmed her memory: it was a series of metal tubes, connected by some kind of mesh. The water was rich with dwemer; their dome had capped the main vents, but dwemer trickled out from a number of smaller ones here and there throughout the reef.

She and Kin had stayed near one of the side vents for a time, but the competition was too fierce. The ravagers and daggerfish were voracious and relentless, and all the cuttlers vied for the few remaining safe hideouts. They might have survived for a while, but communion would have been impossible.

"I'm ready." Kin's bright mind-voice gave Sef a glimmer of hope that this impossible plan might work, that they might get their home back.

"Meet me at the triple shells when you're done," she said as she released him. *"We'll check in with the humans after."*

The circles around Kin's eyes glowed red for a moment, then he took on the color and texture of the pipe as he flattened himself against it. He winked at her, then turned and gazed up at the platform. Sef turned her face down and swam alongside the pipe into the depths.

Sef almost gave up when she saw it. The steel dome lay amid a wreckage of broken, bleached coral. Aside from a few tube worms, nothing remained in the wasteland around the dome. Farther away, parts of the reef remained, fed by the minor vents, but their colors were less vibrant, their bioluminescence much diminished by the lack of dwemer. Her hearts broke to see the devastation up close.

The dome itself was a ravager's length wide; there was no way it could be lifted, even if all of the creatures of the reef pitched in at once. Her plan was impossible and could only lead to her death, and the death of many others, cuttler and osmo alike. But what choice did she have? At the rate they consumed dwemer, the humans would be back for the smaller vents, and the other vents on other reefs, to feed their insatiable hunger. There was no future for her or her kind if they simply let that happen. And if Kin was willing to risk his life on a similarly impossibly mission up above, she *had* to try.

She positioned herself on the thick connector where the pipe led out of the dome. If her call summoned a ravager by accident, at least she might be able to make her death count. She wrapped herself around the connector and camouflaged her body to match. She scanned the water for cuttler waves and picked up several, though they were weak, and probably distant. Still, with the dwemer still flowing through her from draining the tank, she should be able to reach them. She dug deep to summon the call for conclave, which she had neither sent nor heard in quite some time, then sent a single pulse out into the depths. After a pause, she sent another, and another. She got a ping back on the fourth. She went silent, letting them come to her.

Three cuttlers joined her, one trailing her mate in her skirt. One she knew, another she recognized; the third must have been from another reef. No matter. Sef put on her most majestic deep red, assuming the leadership role, and the others went blue in agreement.

"I'm Sef, and this reef is my home. Our home. Tonight, we're going to take it back."

Little dots of pink bloomed in the others' blue, but flecks of yellow crept in.

"How?" It was Pai, whom she'd known since she was a little flailer.

"By risking our lives." Sef did not intend to play down the danger. *"But I don't need to tell you they are at risk already."*

The third cuttler, the one she didn't know, ringed her eyes with red. *"I'm Jo, and with you."*

"I'm in." Pai's eyes flared red as well.

The other one's blue was dotted with yellow. Her mate pulsed out of her skirt, eyes ringed red. He hovered near her eyes, awaiting her decision. He'd made his feelings clear. *"I'm Ni. Laz and I will listen to your plan,"* she said after a long pause, *"and then decide."*

"Fair enough." Sef paused, sending out a sounding pulse, which detected no large moving objects, but they couldn't sit here exposed for too long. *"Let's discuss below."* She shot off toward a space formed by a dead wall of coral that had fallen against another in the shock zone around the foot of the dome. They expelled a group of skinner crabs that were tearing apart a chunk of rotted leviathan and huddled together, with Laz stuck to the top of Ni's head.

"We're going to need our osmo cousins to make this work." Sef glanced from eye to eye; some cuttlers saw osmo as little more than food, but not much separated the species. Sef had even managed to communicate with osmo on occasion, when they hadn't fled at the sight of her. Her plan relied on their intelligence as much as anything. None of the cuttlers showed signs of objection.

She laid out her plan as quickly as possible, sending out visuals of how she imagined everything going, including best- and worst-case scenarios. There was a long pause after she finished, as everyone digested the information. *"We already crippled their processing machine in the city. If this works—if we take this thing out—we might be able to keep them off our reef for some time."*

"Or they might come back with more platforms, more tubes, more domes." Ni's yellow dots remained, but they were shifting orange. *"On this reef and elsewhere."*

"You think they're not planning that already?" Sef spread her skirt wide and let her tentacles glow gold for a moment. She needed to establish dominance. *"If we do nothing, they'll do it faster, to every dwemer reef in the bay and beyond."*

Ni went dark for a moment, then burst out red all over. *"We're in."* She returned to her dark blue, but her eyes were ringed with thick circles of red. Her mate's tentacles flared red as well; he was spoiling for a fight. Sef's hearts swelled, thinking of brave little Kin up above, all alone against an army of humans and their enormous machine.

"Then we're agreed," she said, her red shifting to blue. *"I'll put out the osmo call. Once they start arriving, the ravagers won't be far behind."*

At the word ravager, everyone's tentacles turned red, and their eyes were shot through with blue streaks. Sef returned to black, except around the eyes. Some traditions had to be respected, despite the risk.

"I'm moving into place," she said. *"Be ready."*

Sef circled the dome, camouflaged in deep-sea black. Several dozen osmo of various species had answered her call and were draped over the edges of the dome, all matching its color and texture. Their color communication was a bit different from that of cuttlers, but there was enough in common for Sef to believe they'd understood the plan. Seeing the intelligence and bravery of these cousins, whom so many of her kin dismissed as lesser beings, stirred her hearts and gave her hope. Not just for the success of her plan, but for the future of the reef: a future in which osmo and cuttlers found common ground and protected the reef for all its inhabitants. Even the ravagers, who had as much right to exist as any of them. Especially if they played their role tonight.

Sef linked minds with the cuttlers, who awaited her command with fear-tinted vigilance.

"Put out the call."

Sef sent hers out first, a plaintive sonic wail that would travel far beyond the reef, given the dwemer that still flowed through her from draining the tank. The others followed suit, sending theirs out in different directions, as planned. Sef's hearts ached at the sound, which usually signaled a badly wounded or dying cuttler. She hoped not to hear it again tonight.

The osmo began wriggling in response; the call must have hit them deep as well. When their call stopped, the osmo started flashing red, in sequence, as instructed. Each one stayed red for only an instant, creating the illusion of a red osmo or cuttler circling the dome.

Sef's pads tingled at the first hint of the ravagers' approach. She passed the tingle on to the others through their ambient connection, and they took their positions on the dome, just a few body lengths up from the osmo. Nervous energy crackled between them. The osmo must have felt it too; they glowed fiercely now, a coruscant red that would draw a ravager's attention from far away.

"One incoming," Pai said, panic seeping into her words. *"Make that two...three."*

Sef sent Jo and Ni to join Pai, leaving Sef by herself to watch the other side. The rising tension in their minds indicated the rapid approach of the pod of ravagers. She was tempted to go help them, but a sudden dwemer surge in her pads told her more were coming, using the reef as cover.

"I've got company," she said, bracing herself against the unknown number approaching through the reef. All was quiet for a long moment, then the water boiled with sudden activity. A flash went off behind her, and the dome shook with the vibration of a great blow, then another, and a third. The dome skidded a couple of tentacle lengths across the seafloor, kicking up a storm of dust and debris so dense that she couldn't sense the other ravagers until they were almost upon her. She flashed with all her might and shot upward an instant before they hit. Two landed glancing blows on the dome, and the third hit it dead

on, sending it skidding several tentacle lengths in a different direction. Ink and blue blood filled the water as the ravagers' teeth raked the water, slashing and gobbling those osmo unable to get out of the way in time. Even blind, the ravagers found their prey.

The waters swirled in the wake of the great ravagers, who sped off, no doubt to return to attack en masse. Sef eyed the position of the dome and summoned her tentacled army to the side closest to the where its center used to be. Pai's signal was weak; she'd lost several tentacles and had a series of cuts atop her head, but her eyes were ringed red as lava. A half-dozen of the osmo had been killed, but most grouped together again as Sef directed. She had just started to send out a message to all of them when her pads tingled with the approach of the ravagers.

"Brace yourselves," she managed as the ravagers approached in a group, now ten strong, toward the flashing red and black mass of the osmo. Sef thought of Kin, hiding somewhere on the platform, awaiting her signal. There was no time to send one as the dark shapes of the ravagers careened against each other in

their rush toward their prey, so she spoke directly to the osmo. *"Now!"*

Sef flashed in time with the other cuttlers an instant before her world was thrown into chaos. The force of the ravagers' blows knocked the dome backward and flipped it, scattering cuttlers and osmo in all directions. Ink, blood, and sand filled the churning water as the ravagers hacked their way through the clouds, slicing off tentacles and ripping bodies in half. Instead of darting away to attack again, they began circling, thrashing blindly in every direction. Searing pain shot through Sef's lower half as a ravager latched onto the edge of her skirt and shook its head side to side. She filled its mouth with ink and drifted to the bottom, missing two tentacles and bleeding through a jagged tear in her skirt.

The pain gave way to a strange clarity as the water filled with dwemer, the rich, fresh taste of home. They'd done it. The dome was off, the tube severed; their vent was free again. She perked up in time to shoot out of the way as a ravager churned through the sandy bottom, missing her by a suction cup's breadth.

She shot upward, out of the cloud of blood, ink, and body parts, and sent a wave up to Kin: *"Now!"*

Either her call or her blood must have triggered the ravagers; three of them emerged from the inky cloud and surrounded her, all teeth and murderous eyes. So, this is the end, she thought, strangely calm now that her fate was no longer in question. At least she'd saved the reef, for now. She spread herself wide and flashed her most dazzling pattern, pinks pulsing through purples, reds, and all her other colors from her head down to the tips of her remaining tentacles. This display wouldn't fool a ravager for long, but if she was going to die, it should be in the full glory of her beauty.

The ravagers paused, studying her. More emerged from the murky cloud below; she was surrounded by six now, then eight—all but the two that lay stunned or dead on the ocean floor, along with the mangled bodies and bits of osmo and cuttler alike. She kept up the pattern, which seemed to have kept them at bay for the time being, then summoned all her mental strength to create a glowing picture on her skin. She drew coral of many colors, loaded with anemones and sponges; firebits flitted between them, chased by rockheads. Tentacles draped out beneath her eyes, which served as holes in the coral. At last, she drew the giant shape of a ravager flowing across her, hunting for prey.

The ravagers watched her still, their mouths opening and closing to take in water, but they no longer looked like they were about to tear her apart. Two of the other cuttlers had risen above the cloud, watching. Pai was missing, but there was no time to worry about anything but trying to communicate with the ravagers. She turned her entire body a warm shade of green, uncertain if the ravagers were sensitive to color in the same way cuttlers were; if they hadn't attacked, there had to be a reason. She pushed out a wave of peace and prepared for the worst.

A little green spot glowed on the forehead of one of the ravagers, and the others soon sprouted their own patches of green. The two remaining cuttlers showed their green as well, giving Sef a chance to notice their injuries, which were as bad as hers or worse. Even a handful of osmo floated near them, all the same color of green. Though the taste of blood and death was thick in the water, so was the taste of dwemer. Of freedom. Of home.

Orange light flashed high above, and the water pulsed with the force of a massive explosion like a volcano erupting on the surface.

Kin.

Without a thought, Sef shot away through a gap in the ravagers, who'd turned to face the explosion. She pulsed through the dark depths, fighting through the pain from her bleeding wounds and shredded tentacles. She paused only briefly to look back at the ravagers, who shot up along the pipe, ever eager for their next meal. She sped toward the triple shells, three giant clams stuck together by a colony of barnacles, where she and Kin had agreed to meet.

Had Kin escaped the explosion he'd created? If so, would he escape the notice of the ravagers? Her hearts pumped double time as she scanned the water above for any sign of her beloved. A great groan sounded, followed by another explosion, which lit up the water even from this distance. She saw the pod of ravagers in silhouette, churning toward the surface, but no sign of Kin.

Sef sat atop the shells, gripping tight as she channeled her waning strength into a desperate call: *"KIN!"*

Huge chunks of the platform were now falling through the water, sinking toward the reef. If the whole thing fell, it would cause a lot of damage, but it would be the skeleton around which a new, bigger reef would form. The humans would return, but perhaps the reef's denizens would be more inclined to fight next time. If the ravagers were on their side in this, they might yet keep the humans at bay.

None of this mattered if she lost Kin.

The water was thick with activity, making it nearly impossible to discern the individual creatures moving about. Violent thrashing near the surface indicated ravagers feeding, perhaps on the bodies of the humans thrown from the explosion. It was about time the humans got what was coming to them. The longer she went with no sight of Kin, the angrier and more desperate she grew. So much so that she almost didn't sense the faint call from above.

"Sef!"

She propelled herself off the shells and shot upward, reopening her wounds and leaving a trail of blood in her wake. No matter. Once she found Kin and wrapped him safely in her skirt, she'd take on an army of ravagers to get them to safety.

She felt him at last, a little cone pulsing down toward her. He flashed pink for an instant just before she swirled her skirt around him and tucked him in tight. Her mind flooded with Kin's excitement, terror, and worry.

"You're hurt!" His tentacles lined up along the tear in her skirt, suctioning it together to stop the bleeding. *"Sef, Depths! Are you okay?!?"*

"Nothing that won't grow back, love." She shifted awkwardly into the crevice beneath the triple shells. It was a little tight for her, but she could make it work. It smelled of osmo; if whoever lived here came back from the battle, they'd figure something out. *"I may have lost a couple of tentacles, but I didn't lose the one thing that mattered."* She closed her skirt tighter, though it hurt to do so.

"I don't ever want to be apart from you again."

"And you never will. We'll expand this crevice with a few more shells and make it our home." Even at this distance, she could taste the dwemer in the water, filling her with a sense of security she hadn't known since the humans had capped the vent. It would take some time to recover and prepare for their communion, but they were home again. Soon they would be whole. Soon they would be one.

An odd but familiar vibration reached her from the surface. It was the dwemer boat that had brought them here, but it was speeding in the direction of the flaming platform. Cliff and Seara had probably decided to help rescue whatever humans hadn't been devoured by the ravagers. She couldn't blame them for helping their own. If it hadn't been for them, Sef and Kin could never have pulled this off. She'd promised to let the humans know they were okay, but they'd have to figure it out for themselves. Hopefully, the explosion and the dwemer-filled water would tell them everything they needed to know.

Eighteen

Cliff nursed a mug of redbird tea and reread the latest issue of *Savage Adventures* while waiting for Seara to show. It was about a woman who could turn into an osmo, or possibly an osmo who could turn into a woman; the author left that open. It had some pretty spicy sex scenes, which gave him a chuckle. The whole tentacle thing didn't do much for him, but he could see why people were excited about it. He felt strange reading it in a public place, doubly so in this civilized space where he clearly didn't belong. This was Seara's world, not his. He should be drinking Mae Kambal's tea, weak and a little musty, in his damp tent.

It was nice, though, being treated like a human. All it took was a few marks, and the world was at his feet. If this new maintenance job with the conservancy worked out, he could afford to do this once in a while. Maybe even get a proper roof one of these years, if he could find the right roommate: one who'd tolerate someone like him without *being* someone like him.

"Gods, Cliff, I am *so* sorry." Seara took his hand as she plopped down on the chair across from him, face scrunched with contrition. It was sweet, how she thought she was keeping him from anything.

"No problem at all. How'd it go?"

She sighed as she shrugged off her rain-misted overcoat. "Redbird, hot and frothy," she said to the server, who materialized the moment she sat down. Cliff waved them off; he still had half a mug left. "Honestly, better than I thought it would go, but weird."

Cliff sat up straight at her tone. She'd had a meeting with her boss at the conservancy about the incident, and she'd been worried about losing the job. She'd already dropped to part-time at the plant during repairs, which were expected to take a while. Even beyond that, there was no telling if she'd ever get back up to full time; there would be no bulk dwemer to be processed any time soon unless they diverted it from another capped reef.

"So, I go in there ready to tell him everything. Except for you, of course; no need to drag you into my mess."

"*Our* mess." Cliff tapped on the table for emphasis.

She shook her head rapidly, as if to clear it. "Our mess. Whatever. Point is, no sense getting anyone in unnecessary trouble. But he doesn't ask me what happened. Thanks," she said to the server delivering her tea. She took a big sip, which brought a smile back to her face. "Mmm. I needed that. So anyway, he doesn't ask me what happened. He *tells* me."

"He tells you what happened?"

She nodded enthusiastically. "Yeah. Except, not what actually happened. He tells me what his report to the constabulary says: I went out after dazzler hunters and followed one out into the bay, where they outran me when my dwemer line got kinked. By the time I'd figured out what was wrong and fixed it, it was almost dark. I anchored, planning to sleep on the boat and return at first light. Then the rig blew, and I decided to go see if I could help."

Cliff pursed his lips, tenting his fingers. "It sounds pretty good at first blush. But why is he covering for you?"

Seara smiled over her mug. "That's the best part. Because we helped with the rescue operation, the conservancy gets reimbursed for the dwemer from Stormchain, enough for a full tank, plus my bells, at hazard pay."

"So, you get paid extra for your..." Cliff leaned in and continued in a low voice. "For your *unauthorized* trip?"

"Yeah! And the conservancy gets the dwemer, which would have cost both feet and a hand after what went down."

"He wasn't mad or anything?"

Seara raised her eyebrows and cocked her head. "Part of me thinks he knows what really happened, or some of it. He's a smart business manager, which is why he made sure the conservancy got more than it gave, but also...he genuinely cares. About the reef, about the osmo, about all of it. He goes to court in person for every osmo hunting charge. He's made a few enemies in the business world, but I guess the judges love him."

"When you said he knows, though…I don't see how."

Seara stared out the rain-dappled window, steam from her mug rising into her face. "I've heard him say things now and then at meetings, little asides, like 'The ocean self-corrects when we overstep,' or the way he seems excited for a storm to come in and do some damage. Like he's always rooting for the sea and the creatures in it more than for humanity."

"Can't say as I disagree with him." Cliff swirled the remains of his tea, thinking about Sef and Kin. "I hope it was all worth it."

"It was." Seara frowned into her tea, biting her lip. There was something she wasn't saying.

"But?"

"But losing bells at the power plant was hard. I'm thankful I didn't lose my job at the conservancy, though it only pays half as much per bell as I make at the plant. Rent's going to be tough."

Cliff nodded, studying his tea, afraid to look up into her face. Was she...it didn't seem possible. He didn't know what kind of apartment she had, but it couldn't be very big. And she had her Da to think of. "I'm sure you'll figure something out," he said noncommittally. He dared a peek up and saw her eyes wide with hope.

"That's the thing. I have figured it out." She set down her mug and clenched her hands together in front of her. "My Da sleeps on the couch. His room is...well, it's a bit of a mess right now, but it has a bed. I don't know if..." Seara stared down at her intertwined fingers for a moment, then shook her head with a half-smile. "How would you like to be my roommate?"

Cliff's mouth hung agape as the shock of her words sent tingles across his scalp and down his spine. He hadn't lived with a roof over his head in more than a decade. Hadn't had to pay rent, except the monthly five-mark camp fee, which he didn't mind, since it kept the inspectors off his back. Hadn't had the money for rent in any case. But now, with his new job, he supposed he could—

"I'm sorry, I didn't mean—" Seara closed her eyes and shook her head. "Just forget I said anything. It was a stupid idea, I—"

"Yes." Cliff felt dizzy saying it, but it was a good dizzy, like bubble wine.

Seara gripped his hands, giggling through what looked like the beginnings of tears. "You shouldn't decide right away—you should see the place, and meet Da. He's sweet, he's just—"

"I'm sure we'll have plenty to talk about." Cliff removed one of his hands and placed it atop hers. "Even if it's me doing most of the talking."

Seara's tears flowed for real now, following the lines of her smiling face. It felt awkward to sit there and hold her hand while she cried, especially since he hardly ever touched anyone for more than a moment, but it felt natural at the same time. If the other customers noticed, they showed no signs of it. Seara let out a juddering sigh and withdrew her hands to dry her tears.

"Sorry, it's just...it's been a lot lately."

"I get it." He might not have the same responsibilities as her, but he knew what it was like to fear losing what little you had. He knew what it meant to live in a society that cared little for your welfare beyond what profit you brought it. One that used people up and cast them off once they no longer added to the bottom line. "And to be honest, I wouldn't hate sleeping in a proper bed again."

"Gods, I'm so glad you said yes. You're good people. I didn't want to have to try to find some random person to room with me. There's a lot of bad out there."

"I can attest to that." Cliff's eyes closed as the images of the horrors he'd seen in the camps flashed through his mind. He steered his thoughts back to Mae Kambal, with her ever-present pot of tea, and the water boys who'd serve you even if you couldn't pay them, and the guy who picked up bits of wire and left them outside of Cliff's tent. "But I think there's more good out there than people realize."

"The place is a bit of a mess, but I'll have it cleaned up, I promise. I guess I have time now that my bells at the plant have been cut." She unlocked the door and shouldered it open. "Gets stuck in the jamb when it's humid, which is basically all the time."

Cliff inspected the door; there was a worn spot in the top corner where it stuck. "I could shave that down for you."

Seara dropped her bag by the door and put a finger in front of her lips. "Looks like Da's sleeping," she whispered.

The old man sat on a couch, open-mouthed and drooling, with an old-fashioned Fascinator in his big hands glowing green, then yellow. The couch was covered in blankets, especially under Da. The globe glowed orange, and as it turned red, Da's mouth formed a faint smile, though his eyes remained closed. Cliff turned and followed Seara down a short, dark hallway.

"The kitchen is here," she said in a low voice, gesturing to a space barely big enough for the miniature stove, icebox, washbasin, and chopping block. "It's small, but gets the job done. Kind of like the bathroom." She gestured toward the open door to a room where an undersized bathtub that had been painted over multiple times sat up against a toilet tucked into a corner, with the sink on top.

"You should see the camp latrines." Those were rooms with a dozen holes in the floor, with no privacy whatsoever. You just had to kind of pretend the other people weren't there as you did your business. Even after all this time, he dreaded having to take a shit.

"This is Da's room, though as you can see, he hasn't slept here in several years." The bed was covered in books, and the rest of the room was like a storage closet: pots and pans, mop and broom, a few tools, and the assorted bric-a-brac one accumulated when one had a roof. "I'll have it all sorted before you...I mean, if you decide this is right for you."

"It's perfect," Cliff said. It was no exaggeration. He'd always hated taking up space, and living in a small apartment with two other people felt efficient. "I'll take it."

Seara flashed a wet-eyed smile and held out her hand. As they shook, a voice called from the living room.

"Leila?"

Seara closed her eyes, a forced smile on her face. "My mother. She passed ten years ago." She touched Cliff on the arm and tilted her head toward the living room. "It's just me, Seara," she called cheerily. "I've got someone I want you to meet!"

Cliff followed her down the hall in a haze of warm and confusing feelings. He stood in the doorway as Seara sat next to her Da and gave him an awkward hug, which he returned with one arm, eyes still glued to the Fascinator.

"Dammit, it's blue." He frowned at the globe, then turned his eyes up to Seara.

"Well that gives us a moment to chat, yeah?"

"Is this that fella you were talking about?" He tilted his head toward Cliff without looking at him.

"Yes, Da, it is."

"Green," he murmured, clutching the globe tight. Seara's eyes told Cliff to step forward, so he did.

"I'm Cliff. I work with Seara. It's nice to meet you, Mr. Loewe." He held out a hesitant hand. The old man surprised him by taking it.

"Cliff," he repeated. "Yellow!" His hand slipped from Cliff's, and a glimmer of hope appeared in his eyes. "Are you a fisherman?"

Cliff paused for a moment in surprise. "I used to be."

"Me too. Orange!" He patted Seara on the arm.

"Red is the big event," she said to Cliff with weary amusement.

"You're damned straight it is," Da said with a crooked smile. "Watch! Shh..."

Da's face lit up with joy as the red light washed over him. His open-mouthed smile was contagious; Cliff soon joined Seara and her Da in staring at the Fascinator. It really was a beautiful color of red, rich and full, until it darkened quickly through purple and almost black on its way to blue. Da let out a long rattling sigh and shook his head.

"This is more than he usually talks, if you can believe it." Seara squeezed her father's hand as he sat staring numbly into the deep blue.

"Well, we don't usually have company, do we?" he said without looking away from the globe.

"Sadly true," Seara admitted with a sigh of her own. "Da, how would it be if Cliff moved into your room for a while? He's in between places, and with me losing all those bells—"

Da's bothered wave cut her off. "Fine," he said, staring at the now-green globe. He cocked his head, then turned to look Cliff up and down. "Are you a boyfriend or a roommate?"

Cliff was once again unable to formulate a response.

"Da!" Seara slapped him playfully on the shoulder. "It's not like that. We work together. We're just friends."

"That's good. Yellow!" Cliff's eyes went blurry with tears, and he sat on the couch next to Seara. *Friends.* When was the last time anyone had used that word to describe him? Since becoming unhoused, he'd built a cocoon of solitude around himself. He didn't want anyone from his old life to know how he was living. How he'd failed.

He hadn't talked to his mother or his brother in years. They probably thought he was dead. It was better that way. He kept only as many acquaintances as required to function in the camp, and they all knew he liked to be left alone when possible. It was easier, less messy with no one to let down. But as the warmth from Seara's words flowed through him, his heart burned orange, then glorious red in time with the Fascinator.

When it returned to purple, he sensed Da's disappointment, but Cliff liked the cool part of the cycle. As the colors drifted from purple to blue to green, he felt like he could just be, with no pressure to be more than he was, and no one to make him feel lesser.

It might not last forever, but for now, this felt like home.

Nineteen

Kin danced with excitement as he saw the boat approach. It wasn't the dwemer boat they'd taken out to destroy the rig; this was a small craft, powered by oars, like the one Seara had been in when they'd first met her. He felt her aura from far away; he was flush with dwemer now that the vent had been uncapped. The reef had a long way to go, but it was starting to feel like home again. The humans had come diving for parts of their fallen rig, but the ravagers had put an end to that. Kin still wasn't sure if they understood what they were doing, but they hadn't been feeding on cuttlers, as far as he could tell.

Kin glommed onto Sef's head as she floated over to greet the boat. Seara stood looking into a small device, possibly a seeing tube. She set it down carefully and knelt at the edge of the boat as Sef approached. Kin scurried along her tentacle and onto her pad as she raised it out of the water. The man on the oars held still, his mind as impenetrable as a stone. For whatever reason, he didn't seem to be able to communicate like Seara and Cliff.

"Sef! Kin!" Seara's speech was so natural, it almost felt like she was a cuttler herself. Kin gripped the boat's rail and climbed aboard, wrapping a tentacle around Seara's extended fingers. *"I knew you'd make it out."* Her face contorted as she looked into the water. *"Sef, you're hurt."*

"I'm fine." Sef's two lost tentacles were growing back quickly thanks to the ready supply of dwemer, but they were still a sickly pale color; her outer skin wouldn't grow in for a while. *"Where's Cliff?"*

"He's back home with Da." Her speech warmed as she spoke of him. Were they a mated pair now?

"The reef's coming back!" Kin crawled up her arm to get a close look at her face. Her face distorted in what must have been joy, from the vibes she was giving off. Lacking control of their color, humans seemed to rely

on their faces for much of their communication. *"The ravagers ate the divers who came to salvage the wreck."*

"I heard about that." Her mind grew troubled. *"I'm not sure that's going to keep them away forever."*

"We'll worry about forever when we get there," Sef said. *"Until then, we're going to live for today and tomorrow. Which we can now, thanks to you."* She sent out a potent wave of peace, and Seara's eyes fluttered closed for a moment.

"That's all any of us can do," Seara said once she'd recovered. *"Cliff will be sorry he missed you."*

"Please tell him we said hi!" Kin wanted to wrap his tentacles around her and hug her, but he wasn't sure if humans did that. He stretched a gentle tentacle around the back of her neck, pulling her head toward his until they touched. She was so warm, and her skin had the strangest texture, smooth and grippy but dry, except for a bit of oil. She tasted almost like fresh abalone. One of her hands touched his head, and she leaned into him a little bit. Perhaps humans hugged after all.

"I surely will." She released him, and he crawled back down her arm and onto the railing.

"Maybe you'll see us out here again! We come to the seathorn to hunt sometimes, especially at high tide."

"I'll look for you when the water is up."

Kin's hearts filled with melancholy as he rode Sef's pad below the surface. Would he ever see Seara or Cliff again? He'd long seen humans as callous creatures, only smart enough to be dangerous. While that was true about some of them, there was clearly more to this species than the tales told. He hoped the next humans he met were more like Seara and Cliff than the ones who'd capped the vent.

"With any luck, we won't meet any humans for a long time," Sef said as she swam them back to the reef, Kin tucked snugly in her skirt.

"I hope we do." He was getting sleepy, as he often did while snuggled inside her.

"I love your curious little hearts." Sef's new tentacles hugged him awkwardly; she still couldn't control them fully, so she kept them tucked into her skirt most of the time. Not unlike Kin. Not that he minded; there was nowhere he'd rather be.

Soon, he mused as sleep pulled him under, he would never be apart from her again, as long as they both lived.

They spent their days hunting the now booming reef. Coral, barnacles, and all manner of stationary creatures were jostling to colonize the bounty of the rig's wreckage, bringing goldfin and other delicacies with them. Some of the dead coral had come back, and new patches were cropping up everywhere now that dwemer permeated the water.

The humans' dome had become the domain of a goliath osmo, ten times Sef's size, who'd wrenched off the remains of the pipe with her mighty tentacles and widened the opening enough to let her through. Kin really wanted to meet her, but Sef was adamant that they give her and her dome a wide berth.

"So much for your whole osmo sunshine policy," he'd groused. Sef had been going out of her way to make friends with the osmo. Kin delighted in their playful

spirit, rolling himself up into a ball so they could toss him back and forth among the coral. Of course, Sef hadn't approved, but she wasn't the boss of him. Well, okay, maybe she was, but he was still his own cuttler, for now. Maybe he'd go over there and say hi to the goliath himself one of these days.

He didn't, of course. Communion was almost upon them. Sef's moods had changed; she was clingy, even when they were safely ensconced in the home they'd made out of the triple shells. Sef had found some more giant clam shells and fitted them together with seaweed until the barnacles could grow in. Kin smeared crushed kelp leaves along the cracks to attract their larvae. He enjoyed watching them cluster and grow, a little family on the outside helping make a safe place for Sef and Kin's future family inside. It didn't take the barnacles long to begin colonizing the exterior, cementing the shells together and making this place a real home.

Sef's colors had changed, too; she was more prone to bursts of red and pink, even when hunting. She fed with abandon, gorging herself on schools of goldfin, silversides, even gullies, prickly though they were. After a successful hunt, she'd seize Kin in a tentacle and race back to the triple shells, flaring hot pink with flaming red around the eyes and on the tips of her tentacles. She'd hold him upside down with a pad and stretch his tentacles out one by one with her own, pinning him in place with such strength he could only writhe in anticipation.

She'd wrap a pad around his hecto and squeeze with slow, steady pressure until his tip protruded, desperate for the soft, silky sheath inside her siphon he'd only begun to explore. What he got instead was the tip of her tentacle coiled into a little tube, tightening as he lengthened, suction cups pulling his tip further and further out, like she was extracting the meat from a conch. Kin tried to hold on—he could feel Sef's arousal at seeing him pinned and helpless like this, at her mercy—but when her entire body flared lava-red and her pads squeezed so hard dwemer milk trickled out of her, Kin exploded with ecstasy, filling their little den with the musky taste of his seed.

Kin always tried to reciprocate, but Sef usually refused in her gentle way. "Your pleasure is my pleasure," she'd say, or "I'm saving up for the big day." Kin didn't think it worked that way, but cuttlers were very secretive about what communion actually entailed.

He knew the mechanics of it, more or less; his hecto would extend into her siphon, as far as it could go, and she'd suck his entire body inside her, to a place she'd grown in preparation for communion. What happened after that was a little fuzzy, but their bodies would somehow fuse and their minds grow connected.

Communal cuttlers often spoke as their combined self, but they could speak as individuals as well. Kin imagined there was some jostling for control, some bickering, but he was sure it wouldn't be a problem with him and Sef. If anything, they'd jostle to let the *other* one be in control.

Sef had taken control in most of their sexual encounters of late, but one day, after she'd closed off the entrance to their den, she oozed onto the floor and went deep red all over. Kin tingled from his hearts to the tip of his hecto to see her flip onto her back, exposing the whitish-pink interior of her skirt, the only part of her skin that couldn't change color. Her siphon flared, showing its smooth white interior, luring his eyes to the darkness within. Kin's tip pulsed against its membrane as she stretched her skirt taut and let her tentacles flop, inert, on the sea floor.

Kin fluttered down to land astride her mouth, standing tall on four tentacles while the other four caressed her skirt. She opened her beak wide enough to swallow Kin whole. She ate prey bigger than him all the time, though she usually crushed it to bits with her beak first.

"Let me taste you," she said, sultry as the dusk. Kin looped one tentacle around each horn of her beak, not that he had the strength to stop her powerful jaws. This was about trust as much as it was about the feeling of being consumed. His hecto snaked past these formidable weapons, past her tongue with its rows of jagged teeth, and into the silky terrain of her throat.

As she constricted around him, his tip emerged further and further, bathed in her strength and tenderness. A rumble began deep inside Kin, and he panicked; he couldn't let go so soon, not on this of all days! He pictured a ravager surging up out of the darkness, its eerily transparent teeth glinting in the deep's dim light. That brought him back from the brink for long enough to wrestle himself free of her throat and flop backward onto her skirt.

"Oh, no, you don't." Sef swept Kin up in her pad and pressed him against her siphon, which flared like a ravager's mouth. *"Mama's hungry. Mama needs to eat."* Kin's hearts beat double time at the almost-menace in her tone; she wasn't usually very talky during sex, let alone—

Kin's world was bathed in darkness as she sucked him in and held him tight. Only the top of his head protruded from her siphon. His tentacles were sucked deeper, into a pulsing wonderland of softness. An open space, warmer than the rest of her body, possibly big enough to fit him in his entirety. His suction cups found ducts like the ones in her pad, and a soft, almost sticky spot in the center. He was so distracted by the new sensations and the thoughts spiraling through his mind that he almost didn't notice his hecto moving of its own accord out of the cavity. It found a smaller crevice nearby and probed it; it wasn't wide enough for his hecto to fit very far, but something drew him inexorably inward.

As the crevice narrowed, his tip protruded; it encountered no resistance as it emerged into a tunnel of soft heat. His mind drifted as the crevice tightened, sucking him further and further in. His body was clenched in Sef's siphon, but he perceived it almost as if from a distance, as one might study a bright new sea creature found among the coral.

He watched from above as their consciousnesses merged like two waves clashing in the surf. Whiffs of Sef's concentration, her bliss, rippled through him, along with his own chaotic ecstasy, echoing like a sounding pulse in a cave. His pleasure surged as his tip extended beyond what he had thought it capable of, pulled deep into an unseen world of infinite beauty.

A deep quake erupted in his mind; power surged through him like a dwemer vent bursting through the seafloor to fill the reef with bounty and life. As Sef gripped him tighter still, two of his hearts stopped pumping, and a euphoric tingling raced through his body. He spasmed, inchoate, mind and body reduced to a single point of searing rapture that turned him inside out as she sucked him all the way in.

TWENTY

Kin cruised along the perimeter of the reef, sleek and beautiful and deadly. A sea fan up ahead twitched in an unusual way that triggered a memory: the brush of a crab's claw made the fan move in a specific way. Before he knew it, he was circling around to surprise the unsuspecting crab.

"Quit it, Sef! It's my turn to hunt."

"Sorry! Old habits."

They shared a moment of warmth. It had been hard at first, sharing control, especially since Kin wasn't used to wielding such a large, powerful body. Sef knew he needed a chance to learn, so she let go and kept her focus on the surroundings, in case he missed anything. Between them, they rarely did.

In time, Kin convinced them to make contact with the goliath osmo. They'd seen her come and go now and then; if she'd noticed them, she gave no sign of it. She liked to lurk atop the coral, perfectly disguised down to the barnacles and sponges, and pick off larger fish as they passed. She didn't seem to prey on osmo or cuttlers, as far as they'd seen. And they had to admit she was beautiful.

She proved quite receptive to their greeting, matching their color changes and responding to their dwemer waves with vague waves of her own. They couldn't figure out if she had only rudimentary wave communication or if her language was simply so different that they couldn't understand it. She was quite expressive with her colors and patterns, often reproducing a panoply of reef dwellers simultaneously.

Lacking a way to ask for her name, they called her Anemone. She was quite playful; they stopped by her lair after hunting more days than not. They chased each other around the dome, wrestled, or played catch with a variety of shells she'd apparently collected for that purpose. If Kin were in charge, they'd have stayed to play with her in her dome all day.

When they were almost ready to lay their eggs, Anemone started bringing them fish. The extra feed gave them a lot of energy, which they'd need as they raised their little wrigglers. They plumped up with the help of the extra food and dwemer afforded by these delivered meals.

One evening, they awoke feeling sluggish. At first, they thought they might be sick, but as the pressure built inside them, a sense of panicked excitement spread through them. Their home in the triple shells was in pretty good shape, but there were still holes big enough for a wriggler to slip through. They collected what few shells they could without leaving their den and wedged them into the openings they could find, hoping it would be enough. They should have been more meticulous in their wriggler-proofing, should have thought of everything—were they even fit to be a mother?

A burning need deep within swept away this thought. Kin was dimly aware of the egg bubble passing through a canal next to where his vestigial body lay nestled in her cavity. Relief washed through them as the bubble squirted out with a painful *pop*. Their pads quickly caught the eggs, which were held together by gummy slime, and their tentacles immediately began weaving them into a festoon. Though they'd never witnessed this process, their body knew what to do, and soon they'd woven them all together in a pattern so intricate they doubted they could have figured it out with both their brains working the problem.

There were twenty-three eggs, a little lower than average; perhaps it was because their residual dwemer levels were low from their long time away from the reef and the energy spent healing. They coiled the festoon and set it inside a half-open clam shell, which they covered with another and tucked into their skirt. Even the small fish that sometimes found their way into their den were a danger. They would protect their eggs at all costs.

Anemone continued bringing them fish. She'd put one big eye near the entrance to their den as if to see if anything had hatched. Kef thanked her and even opened the clam shell to show the festoon, at which point Anemone went blue-green all over. Other cut-tlers came by to check in on them as well, giving tips and telling reassuring stories of brood successes. Several moons came and went before they felt the telltale vibrations from within their skirt. They pulled the shell out carefully and opened it to watch the miracle unfold.

Inside each of the transparent pink eggs, a dark shape wriggled. One of the eggs burst, releasing the tiniest cuttler they'd ever seen. Kef's pad caught it, holding it up to one eye to study it. It went pink for a moment before drifting down to land on one of their ducts, which had already begun to leak dwemer. It latched on, its tiny beak tickling as it struggled to suck out the dwemer.

The others began to hatch now, popping out one by one. At this stage, it was impossible to tell male from female, not that it mattered much; most that lived long enough would eventually end up as one, as Sef and Kin had. Some darted right into their pads, but others flitted around aimlessly until Kef's tentacles guided them into place. Before long, they were all safely held in their pads, which Kef closed around them.

As the dwemer flowed into these tiny, helpless beings, Kef's body and mind flushed with bliss. Against all odds, they had saved their reef and found a safe place to become one. The moons to come would be full of fatigue and worry as they fought to keep their brood thriving, but the communion they had found together was the most durable of magics.

FIN

Acknowledgements

Huge thanks to my editor Chris Zable, who not only helped hone the prose but also made sure the fantasy science made sense compared to real-world science.

Thanks to my crew in The Fragrant Rose, including but not limited to May, Tris, Soph, and Sylvia.

Most of all, thanks to you, dear reader, for taking this odd little trip with me into the unknown depths. You are the reason I write.

Also By Dani Finn

The Maer Cycle (*Hollow Road, The Archive,* and *The Place Below)*, a classic fantasy trilogy with LGBTQ characters. It tells the story of the encounter between humans and the legendary hairy humanoids called the Maer and the struggle for the two peoples to reconcile their history and their future.

The Weirdwater Confluence duology (*The Living Waters* and *The Isle of a Thousand Worlds*) are a pair of romantic fantasy books with meditation magic. They are independent of the trilogy, but there are little connections. Both books are sword-free and death-free, in sharp contrast to the Maer Cycle.

Unpainted is a standalone arranged marriage fantasy romance set in the Weirdwater universe, and *The World Within* is a standalone trans sapphic fantasy romance that includes some of the characters from *Unpainted*.

Grey Angel, a T4T lesbian monsterfucker romance set in a new world.

The Time Before: *The Delve, Jagged Shard, Wings so Soft,* and *Cloti's Song,* a group of linked romantic fantasy standalones set 2,000 years before the Maer Cycle. Meant to be read before or after the other books, they tell the story of the fall of the great Maer civilization of old.

Scrublands: A new Switzerland-inspired, western-themed fantasy world. *They of the West* is a novella of friendship and self-discovery about two teens who go chasing after treasure in forbidden canyons.

Short stories:

The Winnie & Crela series, starting with *Barrow Maid,* a lesbian ghoul-necrologist romance;

The Incorporated States series: *User Not Found,* a trans lesbian dystopian censorship tale, and *Iris,* a sci-fi billionaire forcefem story;

Fly by Night, a trans lesbian butterfly-moth romance; and

The Last Solstice Gift, a family vignette set in the Time Before, featuring characters from *Wings so Soft* and *Cloti's Song.*

About the Author

Dani Finn (they/them) is a nonbinary fantasy romance author who occasionally writes fantasy without romance as well.

They favor high-steam love stories that crisscross the gender spectrum, from swords and sorcery to sword-free fantasy with meditation magic and everything in between.

You can find their books, contact information, and other links on their Linktree!